Early Praise for
AMBER EYES

Amber Eyes is an entertaining and heartfelt read centered on the complexities of love, family, societal expectations, and self acceptance. The story starts slow, taking time to introduce the main characters and paint the scene (with some clever recasting of historical events). The pace picks up in the second half, with plenty of romance, conflict, and supernatural elements keeping things compelling. The author has put a great deal of humanity in these characters and leaves a world of possibilities for where they'll go next.

—Steve Jones

The story of Thaddeus is an amazing read. Through the twists and turns of the mythology and supernatural beings, his journey unfolds. I enjoy reading fiction/fantasy, and this book held my attention throughout. I eagerly await the next adventure of Thaddeus and friends.

—Deb Wirth

The characters are inviting, and you can't help but love and hate them. A nice new twist to the fantasy genre. Cannot wait to read again and again!

—Jackson Secor, avid reader

AMBER EYES

An early account in the life of Tyler J. Azuzels

ELI PRITZL

www.ten16press.com - Waukesha, WI

Amber Eyes
Copyrighted © 2022 Eli Pritzl
ISBN 9781645383925
First Edition

Amber Eyes
by Eli Pritzl

For information, please contact:

www.ten16press.com
Waukesha, WI

Art Director: Kaeley Dunteman
Cover Designer: Resa Strasser
Editor: Jenna Zerbel

For Amy. Thank you for supporting this endeavor.

&

In loving memory of my father. He did not see the completion of this project but encouraged and cheered me on for every step of the way.

Trigger warning: derogatory language, sexual content, profanity, and historical terms that are no longer appropriate.

PROLOGUE

The fear of everything that goes bump in the night is conceptualized and visualized as a creature of gangly proportions—hunched over, bloodthirsty. You might imagine it stalking you from the shadows with only its eyes to be seen from the darkness, from the shrouded corners of this world. This concept has undoubtedly come from eons of not knowing what makes things occur in the way they do in this world, or perhaps from the sheer incapacity to understand that oneself is not the most important living thing. Entitlement without due reasoning causes the simple, mundane mind to believe that such a creature would be uncivilized, feral, unholy and damned by God himself. Whilst the creatures they damn are similarly simple creatures as they are, still the human beings consider only themselves worthy of souls. They alone are competent, and no other beast could be capable as such, despite coming from the same origins of cave dwelling.

Creatures that are categorized as supernatural, in the modern age, are either romanticized or cast off—presumed to be nothing more than glowing eyes in the night, waiting for you to fall asleep and consume the idealized humanity. This notion of idealized humanity is a quality that humans alone are entitled to at birth, that no other beast who clings to the earth or breathes its air can embody.

This account of my own travels and occasional wanderings confirms some of these romanticized or damned premonitions of these creatures, though denies most. Those creatures who are cast off from all of humanity and are believed to be beyond redemption of the soul, in fact possess qualities worthy of salvation. With my story, I wish to bring light to the shadows, revealing that the assumed bloodthirsty eyes are merely a trick of the mind, light from a distance or perhaps even swamp gas. These are not beasts, but a manifestation of wayward thoughts.

Beginning a story is much easier said than done; pinpointing the exact moment where it begins becomes an ordeal in itself. What contributing factors were in motion, taking place before my own story began? What must be laid out so as to understand my abundant emotions, interpretations and raw understanding firsthand? Could a history lesson suffice? Hardly, as my understanding of history is much different than what you have been led to believe. A difference of circumstances gives each their own interpretation of knowledge; neither party is entirely right or wrong, merely misinformed of what their stance completely means. This being the case, I can only give my own account, which will differ greatly from your own. Though I promise, it will be told with the truth as I know it to be.

I suppose an accurate place to begin my story could be what preceded my childhood and would ultimately result in my life. These events are what transpired prior to the hellish adolescence I endured, which plagues my thoughts and causes sleep to evade my grasp in my adult life. Here, I do believe I should mention that concepts such as "childhood" or "adulthood" are loose terms to be applied to my own self and many others, as in due time you shall understand. My application of time is far removed from a human's—or a *mundane*. That is, a term that those of us who bear supernatural lineage use for the Homo sapiens.

It is of note that my species does not age like a mundane, nor do we necessarily have a definite life span. Around the age of physical maturity—which does vary between the sexes and individual—our internal clocks slow to an inordinate crawl. Decades could pass, yet not a single aging line would appear. At just over a century old, my mother appeared as a bonny young lass. Likewise, my father hardly appeared a day over thiry years, but he was in fact over three-hundred years of age when I was born. If you took a survey, I do not suppose you would find old age as a cause of death for anyone in my species throughout history. Tragic accident, murder or death at the hands of humans would always occur before the declining years could manifest as means to an end.

My process of coming into existence was the same as any other, however. As previously stated, I had a mother and, regrettably, a father. From the few memories I have of my mother—that without a doubt I hold most preciously in my heart—I know she loved me with her entirety. I remember her hands, soft and gentle as they ran through my unruly hair. A voice that soothed me when my bones would break, when the fever of my transformations scorched my brow and ripped my skin.

I've been told through the centuries, and know quite well firsthand, that I share her fair features. From her I inherited my olive-toned skin, eyes the color of golden honey, and hair as white as midday ocean caps. It hung in beautiful curls around her face when it was just us together—as otherwise, by my father's strict word and hand, she was forced to keep it pinned up underneath an ebony wig. She would lay my head upon her lap as she sang lullabies of her tribe to me, whispering secrets and long-ago tales passed down through the alphas of her ancestors.

She came from the New World to the Old—a descendant of alpha creatures, lethal in their regality. My mother's people were one with nature, changing at will to animals of any shape or form. Their imagination was the only limitation to what shape they could take. They were considered sacred entities by the native peoples who lived among them. These worshipped deities, in a broader and more modern term, are known as shifters. They are the creatures who can walk the earth, appearing as human or as beast.

Long ago, these ancient bloodlines had split between the Old and New World. This commonly occurred in many species, not just my own breed, when ice bridges connected the continents. Ethnically diverse groups—more modernly known as Norsemen celts or pre-Vikings—traversed over these bridges. mundane history recalls them only staying for brief periods, but my mother's people remained in the shadows of that world. The result was divisions within in the Old World—primordial lines of creatures that roamed and created their castes, separating the weak from the strong, becoming kings and queens and gods of their own lands. This was absent in the New World. I often imagine the surprise of my sire's family upon receiving word from missionaries, having stepped foot in the New World with the intent to conquer it, that a family just as powerful and old as their own was present. More powerful, in fact, and they already had this New World within their grasp.

It was this contact of archaic families that sealed my mother's fate. My birth was inevitable—as well as, ultimately, her death in my youth. Hers was a death mourned by few, but the Earth itself seemed to weep on the macabre day when she drew her last breath.

This wretched day transpired without a word from her supposed husband—a union born from an agreement between old families, as kings and queens so often created with the intent of a forging alliance through matrimony.

The union between my parents was many things, but it was never held sacred. My father came to be the head of his family, the alpha, through an ode to Roman betrayal—poison and backstabbing. He killed his own father with the simple reason of greed. Though I never knew my grandfather, his poetic murder having been committed a few hundred years prior to my birth, I often believe we would have gotten on better than I do with my other relatives, who even now wish for my death. They all want to rid the world of the blood of my mother, which runs through my veins.

The *pack* is a term with dual meaning in my story. It means either a family of blood relation or, as often is the case in this supernaturally riddled world, a collection of creatures that behaves as one family unit, regardless of blood or affiliation to the same species. One of the most powerful packs is the Avalone family, of which my father, Cenric Avalone, is the alpha.

Unfortunately, my knowledge of my sire's history is slim, as in the time I did reside in his household it was not knowledge I was permitted to know. Although I was heir, it was a vacant title, for many others would not stand to see my mixed blood in a position of power before their own. Though both my lines of lineage were purely of the shape-changing blood, the English breed viewed any creatures from the New World, although similar in nearly every way, as heathens.

The average, mundane recollection is correct with regard to the way things stood among creatures behind the supernatural curtain so long before contact with the Americas. They were persecuted relentlessly. Not in every place, of course. Take the North, for instance, where the God of Thunder dominated the sky. Such creatures—who do not make an appearance in this recollection—were not hunted so. Rather, they were revered as lesser deities.

Cultures you can recall, whose stories are repeated with enthusiasm, were in fact some of the safer lands to dwell in. Those other lands, however, where one god ruled above the sheep that feared the wolf in its borrowed fleece...these were the lands where creatures would be bled.

To adapt, the ancestors of my sire's line learned incredible self-control, to bridle their outer appearances and behaviors. Steadily throughout the centuries, they would rise to those noble palaces of royalty, slaughtering those who might be suspicious of their position. The Avalone family is but one of many that accomplished this, but they were smart enough not to take the position as regent. Instead, they aimed for positions as trusted advisors, those who dealt directly with politics.

They hid themselves well, keeping their appearances mundane. The surname is commonly associated with hair black as coal and eyes to match, only having a faint glow within the exact right light of a candle. Held high were the heads of the Avalones, so prideful of their lineage. No one can truly hide what lies behind their own eyes, for they are windows to one's soul, and in theirs I only saw malice.

My mother's soul, contrary to my father and pack alike, could only be described as pure. Because of the few, clouded memories I can recall, the resemblance I bear to her is but all I know personally of her. Tales from others have surfaced over the years, and thus I have managed to put together an incomplete understanding of her life before parting from this world.

Josephine—a name forced upon her by my father—was leader of her tribe for a short time (that is, in proportion to our exceptionally long life spans). My mother's reign was just shy of one hundred years. Her pack was small, containing only a handful of other shifters who would later perish, and thus I have never been able to meet them. Her people were those who belonged to the earth, worked her soils and lived alongside her in nature. To their own they kept, leading secluded lives. They were viewed as elusive totems or spirits, rare with incredible beauty that would bring one luck if they were able to view it. Benevolent in demeanor, the creatures known in the New World as *skinwalkers* were, in short, something of fairy tales, known real and revered.

How they revealed themselves was how they naturally appeared. Skinwalkers did not hide features of their natural state (with the common exception of the human children who stumbled upon them, so as to prevent petrifying the little ones) and had a wide variety of unique characteristics. This was contrary to my father's line, who evolved to have suppressed traits and appear mundane. My mother's own ancestry remained ethereal in appearance, and so does mine, though to a lesser extent. I inherited her untamed white hair, a tail to match, elongated canines and something I never have been able to cloak—amber, catlike eyes. Such features, though feral, lead to an undeniable beauty, and in the beginning of my parents' relationship, these features were what drew my father's drifting eyes and aided in his willingness to copulate with what he saw as a lesser being.

The Avalones encountered my mother's pack in what is now known as Canada. My sire's family had a hand in nearly every enterprise, with intent to dominate wherever they trod. Fur trading was one such event. Montreal is where my mother had the unfortunate luck of being spotted by an ambassador of my father's company. Stories had circulated among supernatural beings of new creatures that were all but impossible to find.

My mother's people were unpredictable, openly displaying their supernatural traits that could, in my sire's opinion, expose his pack's well-protected secrets. She was spotted in a market—and though she was bundled up with her hair hidden, my mother's inhuman eyes and scent alerted the lowly spy, who quickly sent word back to London of her discovery. As immediately as was possible during that age, those closest to my father were sent out. Men were sent—trackers and ambassadors alike—possessing full ability to hunt down the New World pack.

With silver tongues that enticed her with words and false promises, they led my peace-seeking mother abroad, bound for London. Josephine had adventure in her blood, but her slowly evolving understanding of how the Old World treated supernatural creatures soon made it clear that she had made a mistake. She knew her only option for protection was to agree to marry the head of the Avalone family—Cenric Avalone, my father.

As aforementioned, this was a common trading practice between families of power. What she gained was an offer of protection for her tribe and an opportunity to let her wild heart explore this Old World. She could not have known, however, that it would only result in misery, as well as the death of her line and pack. the final result was my own life.

Here is where I do believe my own story can begin, having now conveyed sufficient background information regarding what is hidden in your world.

CHAPTER 1

I became a man in the year 1758. At dawn on the eighteenth anniversary of my birth, alone I watched the sunrise break over the horizon of London through my window. I sat up in bed, the blanket sliding down from my shoulders and pooling around my waist.

The first rays of the sun trickled into my room, the stained glass of the window casting shimmering refractions of light onto the walls and floors. I brushed my white hair back over my scalp and away from my face, blinking away the lingering prickle of sleep. My mind cleared, and a moment of peace washed over me as I got lost in the beauty of this sunrise. This brief moment alone was all I would have for the day, given the planned festivities, so I quietly enjoyed my own company.

London often had a mist over her, clouds heavy with rain. Today, though, the sun's rays had broken through. The weather would be perfect and sunny. A small smile spread across my face, knees tucking up under my chin as I continued to gaze out over the scenery. Everything was quiet—a seemingly frozen moment—and only my breathing signified that time was not, in fact, standing still.

A knock at the door drew my attention, my golden eyes watching as the door opened slowly. Then my personal attendant, Jacques, entered the room.

"Good morning, young lord," he quietly spoke.

Dressed for the day, Jacques was cloaked in black, from his shirt and vest, his britches down to his shoes—our servants' uniform. Walking toward me, Jacques held a small cup of tea in hand and placed it upon my bedside table before clearing his throat.

"The festivities for your birthday are set to commence at noon, though I do anticipate arrivals to begin around ten."

I nodded, acknowledging I had heard his message and that he could continue. My gaze wandered back to the window and to the city spread out over the horizon. Jacques continued to run through the morning's itinerary as I unhurriedly sipped from the porcelain cup. Its steam curled up around my nose, while the heat radiating from that delicate cup caused my fingers to take turns dancing on the surface. Another small dish manifested beside my saucer, and upon it were three delicately placed pastries—simple, just as I had requested the night before. Popping one into my mouth, I found that it was moist and had the fleeting taste of vanilla—easy on my stomach, perfect in its simplicity.

"Once you have finished breakfast, I would suggest bathing and dressing straight away, sir." Jacques' heels clicked against the wooden floors as he opened drawers of the chiffonier and placed undergarments on top of the furniture. Next, he moved to the closet, pulling out a blue suit that had been prepared the day before. "Your bath is already drawn, sir, and I urge you to move into the next room as I prepare your clothing."

With a sigh, I set the teacup down, swinging my legs over the side of the bed. The banyan I wore tumbled around my ankles as I rose, and I stifled a yawn with the back of my hand. The chill of the floor crept into my toes, and a bath really did sound inviting. What a perfect way to shake myself of this morning numbness. I walked into the neighboring bathroom, shedding my clothes. A small shiver ran through me as the bath's steam enticed me.

Testing the bathwater proved what I already knew—it was at the perfect temperature. One hand clasped the side of the tub as I stepped in, my eyes closing in a moment of indulgence as the water's fever encased me. I slid in, the warmth soaking into my stiff joints, and a groan passed my lips. The scent of lavender hung in the steamy air, and a smile spread across my face. Given the anticipated stresses of the day, Jacques had provided this one last moment of escape for me. I exhaled, beginning to wash my hair, making a mental note to thank him.

Scrubbed clean, I settled into the tub, watching the steam rise into the chilled air. The manor was surprisingly quiet, I observed as my ears perked up above the water's surface. Quiet footsteps echoed through the corridors and passages, likely those of additional servants preparing for the party. Aside from that, I was unable to detect anything but whispers. My arms came to rest upon the sides of the tub, my head against the lip. I closed my eyes with another sigh, trying to mentally prepare myself.

This day had been anticipated by many in the aristocratic and highborn circles. I was finally at an age to be married, and through their daughters, many desired a possible foothold in the Avalone family. Would I have a fiancée at the end of the night? Not necessarily, but my father would no doubt have begun the conversations to negotiate and receive the most laudable dowry he could secure. Such a union, made by payments and bribes, could not be a happy one—of that I was quite sure. I was determined, though, that I would be respectful to my wife-to-be. I would indulge her desires both in society and in private—above all being respectful—in the hope that later in our lives, she might accept a quiet divorce.

All too soon, Jacques' familiar knock stopped my runaway thoughts, and I rose out of the tub. Water cascaded over the muscles of my torso and thighs, and in its wake, a chill nipped at my skin. I'd forgotten for a moment how cool it had been, for the tub's wonderfully sultry temperature masked it. I reached for a towel just in time to cover my person before Jacques entered.

"Come, you must dry yourself off, young lord—lest you catch a cold." He retrieved an additional towel from the linen closet and assisted in drying off my back and hair.

Such a thing might be considered quite peculiar if looking back on it in the modern age, but during those times, at least for those of us in the upper class, this was a very common practice. Jacques had been my personal hand since I was but a babe and tended to me throughout my childhood. My handler produced a robe, wrapping me up. I smiled, realizing he had it heated by the fire, and reached out a hand, placing it on his shoulder.

Jacques paused, looking at me with his same calm expression, "Yes, young lord?"

I let out a small chuckle, my own golden eyes looking into his, tranquil, blue and accepting. "Thank you for this morning," I ran a hand back through my white hair, giving my head a small shake. "The thought of this day approaching has been overwhelming, but at least this peaceful morning you have provided has given me a moment to breathe..." My words trailed off as he gently placed a hand on the top of my head, patting affectionately.

"Young lord, there is no need for thanks. I promised your mother, when you were but a tot, to watch and care for you." His face broke into a proud beam, "It has been an honor, and I do wish to remain in your service, Thaddeus." He ruffled my damp hair again and gained another chuckle from me.

"Aye, me too, Jacques," I affirmed.

With a small nod he held out his arm, wishing me to lead the way back to my room. He made quick work of getting me dressed—first in undergarments, then onto my britches and vest. Everything was in deep blue hues and golden threaded trim. It was meant to be evident with one glance which family I belonged to. With such rich garments, it would be impossible for one to mistake my lineage.

Jacques secured my cravat into place, skillfully adjusting it in such a way that I did not feel as if I were suffocating from its voluminous plume. Just as he did every morning, Jacques stood me before the mirror, giving a small tap to my ears.

"You have yet to remember to do this on your own, young lord," Jacques chuckled. "Although your father has no intention of marrying you into a family of humans, I am sure that there will be some in attendance. You must remain focused on suppressing your extramundane appearance."

"Yes, of course," I confirmed, watching in the mirror as my ears rounded off. I focused to transform, so that I could blend in with the Homo sapiens. Without being further coached, I blinked briefly, my eyes bleeding into a browner tone than their default yellow amber.

Finally, with my subtle transformations complete, Jacques slipped a ring onto my index digit. This ring was familiar to me, one I was required—as most shifters are—to wear at important meetings and events, or any such occurrence where humans were present. Witches had a perfect and quite profitable niche for such charmed items as this apparent family heirloom. This ring would uphold my facade without my needing to focus upon it.

Garmr was the name this ring bore. It was a silver band with two wolves' heads, and within their jaws the main jewel was clasped in place—a cushion cut garnet. Additionally, the eyes of these twin wolves were made of the same stone. In a semblance of a bridle were four accent stones of turquoise, and unbeknownst to anyone but the wearer, engraved within the band were ancient Norse runes that provided the magic of concealment.

I clenched my fist and stretched it out once again, feeling the magic of this ring buzzing against my hand before it settled into its rhythmic pulse of control, which soon was unnoticeable. My observance returned to my reflection, well-polished and appropriately posh for the intended guests and atmosphere ahead. Jacques tended to my hair, lightly brushing it back and tying it with a blue ribbon at the nape of my neck. His hands smoothed down the lapels at my shoulders before he clasped them and gave me a proud grin in the mirror. I returned it, letting out a nervous chuckle. I looked like someone I barely recognized, put-together and tame.

My eye was drawn away by a shadow of movement behind us. As this figure entered the room, Jacques stepped to the side, eyes fixating on a distant point in the room. The man's heavy boots thudded against the floor, coming to stand next to me, and his cold, cynical eyes looked me over, devoid of expression. He wore a general's uniform, medals polished and every manner of his ensemble immaculate. The man's empty title passed my lips, while my eyes locked with his through our lurid picture.

"Father."

CHAPTER 2

A low growl was what I received in acknowledgement, his nose upturning as his tenebrous eyes took in the sight of my presence. My father was a tall and well-built man, commanding an incredible presence as the alpha, and thus head of our family. Once more before that mirror, as I have been so often reminded, I saw plainly how little I inherited from my father. His eyes were small and devoid of light—naturally a dark brown, they appeared almost black. His monochromatic features continued to the greying black hair that was slicked back against his head, and his matching facial hair was impeccably trimmed. Whereas most would lower their stance within his presence, I felt my chest swell, my eyes narrowing as I refused to back down from him. This earned a dreadful smirk from my father and an equally ghastly laugh.

"You have surprised me," he lowly hissed. "It goes without saying that I have never expected much," he chided. "You were so small and so weak when you came into this world, but here we are today."

His frigid eyes drifted over my reflection in the mirror, and I felt a chill seep into my bones at his hateful words. The air within the room seemed as if it were thinning and became suffocating all at once. I wanted nothing more than to bark in his face and gnash my teeth, but scars from previous attempts remained, so I stood stoically. He clearly saw the hate boiling behind my eyes, taking a twisted pleasure in my discomfort as he leaned forward, his breath against my ear.

"And you have become of use to this family after all. You will provide another tendril of access for me." He smirked, straightening up and adjusting his outer jacket. His somber eyes connected with mine, "And you will be mindful to do as instructed this evening, as I do not wish to regret allowing you amongst the noble families. Act congruously, and my favor of your presence may persist."

The muscles of my jaw clenched, and I gave a curt nod in acknowledgement of his words. He tacitly growled, with a delighted smirk plastered onto his face. My skin crawled, to do as much as give this semblance of agreement to the man I was forced by blood to call father. Though forced, my answer seemed to satisfy him.

"And learn to smile, Thaddeus. After today, you will be on the fast track to a married life." He stepped back, brought a wrist up and adjusted his cufflink with a chuckle. "Hopefully, soon you will have your own brats on the way—that is, *if* you are capable of reproducing." He cackled heartily at his cruel joke, turning away from me and towards the door.

I watched his receding stature in the mirror until he paused at the door frame, his voice falling flat and emotionless as he spoke, "Your mother made her mistakes, and she is no longer here because of it. Use tonight as a way to make yourself valuable, or I will not hesitate to dispose of you once and for all, Thaddeus."

Having made his threat clear, he walked through the door without facing me again—his loud footsteps echoed down the halls after him.

I stood before the mirror, finally meeting my own eyes, and let out a shuddering breath as the petrifying atmosphere left the room with him, my eyes burning with tears. I hated everything I saw—a submissive, would-be alpha who believed that man's cruel words. My mind darkened, self-hatred rising to the surface.

A gentle hand slid onto my shoulder, giving it a reassuring squeeze. Blinking away the curtain of darkness for a moment, I realized Jacques had come up beside me, offering a soft smile. This was all he could offer me, unfortunately. Words could not mend the desolate cavity within my chest, and he knew that well.

"Come, young lord. There is enough time before guests arrive, let us walk the gardens," Jacques stated, pulling me away from the mirror.

His hand guided me down the hall, only having to slide off of my shoulder when the voices of other servants came within proximity. My eyes remained fixated on the passing floorboards underfoot, refusing to look up from their walnut strips.

Jacques noticed this and gave my chin a light tap to raise my head, "Look ahead rather than behind, young lord."

His words echoed in my ears, and I heeded them. I raised my head and rolled my shoulders back, nodding in greeting to those we passed. As I often would, I shoved my feelings down, trying my best to do as Jacques said, to look forward. Much of my future would be decided by this day. What use I would be in my family's future, my value solely measured by my usefulness as their pawn— that was obvious before the conversation with my father, but was laid out in black and white thereafter. Even so, the day did offer a new possibility. Arranged marriages were a tactful business and social decision, all placed onto two individuals who wanted no involvement yet found themselves at the center. Some poor lass shared my fate, and our paths were destined to be intertwined starting tonight.

When I walked out of the manor, the sunlight of the chilled morning washed over me. Yet, the air was steadily warming. Today was a new day. Many paths existed before me, and however miniscule my involvement was believed by others to be, I still had a hand in that fate. I never could subject someone to my will, having endured such treatment myself, but I could use tonight to find someone who could be a friend. On this night, I could put forth my best effort to create a friendship with someone who I could prepare to share my life with.

Any and all supernatural families in attendance would be candidates, though plenty of mundane individuals would be in attendance as well to hinder any suspicions. Ultimately, my future wife's family and my father would make the decision, but perhaps a future father-in-law could be pushed to try harder for me if his daughter were willing. From this starting point, maybe it could develop into a stronger relationship or, more likely, conclude with a mutual split decades down the road. Tonight's chance, however, was such that I could have a glimmer of hope for the future, and it was within my power to influence the outcome.

This walk had been the perfect solution. With my head clearing, I possessed adequate optimism for the evening. My heels clicked against the cobblestone underfoot, while I smelled the fragrance of roses all around. The jewel of any noble family was their gardens, and with an inordinate amount of pride, I believed that ours could be the pinnacle of those in London. Vast, well-tended thickets lined the walkway I strolled. A lush sea, its hues of red and crisp white were in bloom. All the bushes of this garden were planted by my mother's hands. It was a self-comforting task she took on, connecting her to the earth and filling her lonely hours. With such love and tender care placed into the soil, the garden burgeoned almost magically overnight, or so I have been told.

These swells of bountiful roses became the envy of every lord and lady of this city. In fact, for this evening's celebration, multiple families without the hand of a daughter to exploit were to attend only to have a glimpse of these enchanting grounds. I carefully extended a rose out from the bush, pulling the bloom to my nose and inhaling the sweet scent. I have few memories of my mother, but here in this place where she managed to create life, I could feel her summery embrace. I released the flower back into the hedges, stepping back and absorbing the sight of the garden in full bloom.

The privacy of the gardens allowed for Jacques' familiar hand to slide onto my shoulder, and I was drawn out of my admiring trance. I let out a mild chuckle and turned to face him. "Again, you have provided exactly what I required. I feel I can face what comes today," I confessed.

Small lines adorned the corners of his eyes as he smiled, letting out a chuckle of his own, gazing up at the flowers before us. "I am glad. Your mother's spirit is still strong and present deep in the soil here." He paused, smiling once more at the scenery. "Since her passing, bringing you here was always the best I could do to provide solace for you. I do believe that spending time here—in nature that she, herself, created—can root you to the guidance she would have given you." As Jacques spoke, he was seemingly lost in his memories. Though he was now my personal retainer, Jacques was such to my mother first.

He was personally hired by my mother, though he was ultimately approved, too, by my father. Jacques was the only individual who was sensitive to her situation and even provided exemplary assistance with her learning English and the proper etiquette to function in this foreign land. He did so in excellent forgery, for while he appeared to be completely loyal to my father, he was anything but. His devotion was to my mother alone.

Like all servants to the Avalone family, Jacques was not human. In fact, he happened to be a scholarly mage—aged a few hundred years before coming into my mother's service. His specialization was in trinket crafting, illusions and related studies. Many would whisper of his intentions in taking such a position. Some rumors suggested that he took it just to get closer to the tight-knit circle that was the Avalone family, while other circulations were as slanderous as to say an affair was occurring between Jacques and my mother.

There is no doubt in my mind, however, that these rumors are simply that. For in truth, what he had was a great intrigue about the beasts from the New World and their magic. I believe that, like many magic users and those devoted to the study of the craft, Jacques was drawn to his choice of employer in order to learn about and study my mother. Befriending her may not have been his anticipated role, but it had occurred, nonetheless.

Jacques was incredibly compassionate and giving, and he had a strong hand in my upbringing after my mother's passing, giving his guidance and wisdom unconditionally—something more substantial than I have ever received from my own flesh and blood. As aforementioned, he was quite a few hundred years older than he appeared, which at the moment hovered somewhere in his early fifties. To say I thought of him like a father would not be entirely true, as my own father was very present and resentfully discordant. Jacques, to me, almost held the presence of an older brother. He was insightful in his ways of instruction, and we did have that sense of kinship. He was my only friend in this suffocating place.

Jacques' attention was drawn to the road leading to our estate, and my own followed. A lone carriage rattled against the cobblestones, though in the distant rolling hills, additional carriages could be seen teetering our way.

"It would seem your cousins are the first to arrive. Shall we greet them, young lord?" Jacques asked.

I sighed, glancing again at the rose hedges around us, inhaling the scent once more and composing myself. "Yes, we most certainly should," I turned on my heel, stiffening my jaw and confidently walking from the gardens.

Tonight, my journey would truly begin—many paths were laid out before me. Years later, I would reflect upon this night, knowing that this is when my destiny changed forever.

CHAPTER 3

Carriages rattled up to the front of the estate, with each lord and lady announced as they emerged, habilimented in their exquisite attires. Though the ultimate purpose of tonight was for my father to scope out a potential engagement for me, as stated before, persons invited to this event included more than simply potential fiancées and their families. My party would also allow all of the socially elite to mingle on any prospect they wished. With such potential in politics and investment alike, deals and contracts would be struck tonight. All the while, participants would flaunt their own level of stature with poise and attire. Though I was lavishly dressed, my own attire could easily be categorized as plain, compared to some. Powdered faces, wigs and perfumes, yards of fabric and ornate jewelry decorated our guests.

Appointed liveried attendants assisted in the descent of our guests from their carriages, gracing the party with their presence in a flutter of fabrics. I was one of the first in line to greet my manifold guests, for the first hour or so. Father, thankfully, had left my side early on and was already engaged in conversation. Jacques remained behind me as a shadow, and with each announced arrival, he whispered to me a few quick facts if they were not intimately familiar to myself.

A particularly opulent carriage clattered over the cobblestone—black exterior adorned with golden filigree, and additional golden detailing on the spokes and metal work. Two black Friesian horses drew the carriage, strong and sturdy beasts that were responsive to their handler and effortlessly brought the carriage to a stop.

"Lord Atlas Charron!" the herald announced as the door of the carriage opened.

Jacques leaned forward, speaking faintly over my shoulder, "Lord Charron is the heir to the mundane carriage company, Charron and Sons. Their company produces top-of-the-line carriages for the royal family and nobles alike." I nodded to Jacques, holding my head up and making sure to smile.

From the carriage emerged a youthful man, similar in age to myself. His blonde hair hung in loose curls around his face, his attractive blue eyes blinking in the light of the sun. He stepped down from the carriage, and his garb was humbler than most but flattering to his stature, which was a hair shorter than mine. I found my tongue going dry, and my heart began to pound in my chest, almost akin to a flutter of anxiety, as the man approached me with a shy twinkle upon his face.

"Happy Birthday, Lord Thaddeus," my guest expressed, with a quirky little simper across his face as he extended his hand to me. Closer to me now, I saw the man had a face full of freckles, his bright shimmering eyes striking deep into my core. He was an attractive man, and automatically my hand reached out and took his, firmly shaking it.

"Thank you kindly, and call me Thaddeus if you like. It is a pleasure to meet you, Atlas," I plainly stated, continuing to shake his hand. The human's eyes seemed to sparkle as he gave a cute nod, causing the curls upon his head to bounce lightly.

"Likewise, Thaddeus. What a wonderful day to turn eighteen. The beautiful weather truly is a blessing," he chirped. He had a slight accent—French perhaps—though he spoke English quite well.

I felt a sense of reluctance as our hands parted, having a desire to continue speaking. I cleared my throat with a light cough, "Yes, the sun has graced us today with its presence, quite a rare thing here in London." I managed a chuckle.

Color rose into the man's face as he gave a hearty howl along with me. "Something rare indeed!" he agreed. His cheeky little smile remained, and he gave me a light clap on the shoulder. "So tell me, has your family made a decision for you yet? My own continues to search for a lass that I am to marry. I've had no say in the whole process!" He chortled, looking up at me with his gorgeous blue eyes.

His laugh was contagious, and I shared in it from the very depths of my belly, using my sleeve to wipe my eyes. It was a comforting relief, almost, that another soul did understand my situation and the black humor of it. We both understood and shared in it.

"Neither do I, though I can venture a few guesses as to certain families who are contenders," I mentioned, holding my chin between my thumb and index finger, the former of which extended up over the tip of my nose in a shushing gesture.

Atlas had been among the last of my guests to arrive, and I decided to walk with him towards the estate to join the party as our conversation continued. Jacques quietly trailed us, though I do believe I caught sight of a soft smile upon his face. I did not have friends, really, and typically was not one who fell easily into conversation. Therefore, my doing so with Atlas was a surprise. My only previous practice was business discussions. Our pace was slow as we walked and engaged with one another. My hands rested against the small of my back, head tilted as I listened to his enjoyable twittering.

"Ah yes, while I have my own suspicions, they are only a guess on my part, as it seems for you as well," Atlas spoke. The August sun bounced off his hair in an illuminating manner, and I was further enraptured. The glint in his eyes and the warmth in his face seemed to capture my attention undividedly. Atlas was indeed charismatic, an encouraging factor that continued our ease of communication.

"That is quite true on my part," I said with a smile. "Though..." I paused momentarily, as we entered the party. Servants passed us by, busily attending to every guest's needs. One came near to us with glistening flutes of champagne on his tray, and after commandeering two, I handed one to Atlas.

"My thanks," Atlas stated, raising his glass to me. I met mine to his, clinking them against one another before we each took small sips. He nodded for me to continue.

The bubbles danced over my tongue as the smooth liquid went down, and I cleared my throat before speaking. "All one can really hope for is that she is easy to get on with," I stated, watching Atlas' reaction.

The blonde was quick to nod, "Yes, most undoubtedly! As I have come to observe from my own parents, a happy wife will make a happy life, my friend!" We raised our glasses to the statement, both throwing back the remainder of our drinks. Atlas was truly an enchanting person, and I couldn't bring myself to peel away from his side—drawn like a moth to the flame, as the saying goes.

The nobles mingled around us, holding their own conversations with one another while a string quartet played in the background, filling the air with their tranquil melody. The atmosphere was light, with drinks plentiful and joyous company all around. Potential fiancées huddled in their own groups, holding catty conversations, either glaring at another woman or yearningly watching myself. Though I took notice, none of it mattered in that moment. Atlas and I engaged in our own conversation that no outside force could seem to penetrate. With ease, we discussed various topics, learning about one another and beginning the foundation of a friendship. Similarly, our families both owned racehorses. This further livened our discussion.

"Thaddeus, we must attend the races together! Oh, when is the next race? A few weeks from now?" He chortled—presumably glancing around for someone who would have the answer—but waved his hand dismissively and turned his attention back to me. "Whenever it is, do you say that you will attend with me? A night on the town of London with other like-minded gentlemen is just what we deserve!"

He clapped his arm over my shoulders, giving my frame an encouraging shake. His touch was easily given, possessing familiarity that can only stem from knowing someone for a long time. Yet, he readily gave it to me, someone he had just met today. Atlas was flirtatious, harmlessly so. Nonetheless, I found myself falling into it myself, not only accepting his behavior, but also feeding into it with my own. It was discreetly done, drawing no disapproving glances or grunts from Jacques at the very least.

I chuckled mildly and nodded my head to the human. "Yes, we must, Atlas," I confirmed by clasping my own arm across his back, the pair of us once more heartily laughing. I had of course interacted with humans before, though strictly from a business platform. The individuals I had met were dull and uninspiring. Atlas was no comparison to them, being so bright and full of life.

A small tug at the edge of my coat drew my attention down and away from Atlas, and I was met with big green eyes brilliantly gazing up at me.

"Hello, Verona. How fare you tonight, cousin?" I tepidly asked.

The petite girl of six held the end of my coat in her small fist. First cousin to me on my father's side, this little coal-haired girl was the darling of our family. It had been centuries since a female had been born to the Avalone family. Thus, many were waiting in anticipation for her juvenescence to cease, to find out her hierarchy marker. A creeping suspense had hung over the family since her birth.

If she were a female alpha, then she would be the only person who could have the right to take my father's currently held position in the pack. He was the younger brother of his immediate family, and his elder brother—now passed—was Verona's father. In the eyes of my father, Verona was a threat—should she present as an alpha and challenge father as head of the family upon maturity. Though, to me, Verona was just my darling young cousin. She was someone I held dear, as well as the only one who I had a functioning relationship with within my family.

The juvenile shifter wore an exquisite blue dress. Its voluminous ruffles and bows made Verona appear like a porcelain doll. The lass beamed up at me and giggled, giving my coat another tug. "Thaddeus, will you dance with me, please? No one else will!" She puffed out her cheeks in obvious frustration.

Without a moment to answer, Atlas—whose arm was still wrapped over my shoulder—gave it a slight squeeze. There was a soft and genuine smile on his face as he looked down towards Verona.

"How the ladies will swoon if you do, my friend," he encouraged, his approval adding another layer of glint to my cousin's eyes. I shared with Verona another smile, as well. I would not have needed to be convinced to join her, but especially now, any residual shyness about doing so had melted away with Atlas' words.

"Of course, little cousin. I would be honored to dance with you," I affirmed, taking her small hand in mine and leading the young girl to the center of the yard, which was designated for dancing.

Verona's face beamed with utter delight, her small feet stepping onto the tips of my own. The music was smooth and mellow, with lords and ladies already dancing slowly around us. The two of us swayed back and forth, effortlessly gliding across the grass to the music. My hand rested upon her upper back to support her tiny frame, and her one hand held mine.

The girl's other arm was wrapped around my leg, and I suppose most of my guests watched us spin together. Whether they observed in judgement or cordial manner was void to me, as I could feel Atlas' blue eyes upon us. My own masked eyes met his as this dance with my cousin began, a captivating grin warming his cheeks with a gentle glow. I returned it, and throughout the dance I would attempt to look away, only to have my gaze reconnect with his soon thereafter. It was almost euphoric, feeling this human's eyes upon me. I could not, however, give a reason for why I felt as such.

Joy—something I had not felt for a long time—pumped through my veins, and I found myself enjoying this event I had dreaded for so many weeks. Verona giggled with glee, giving my legs a tight squeeze as we continued to oscillate. Though, finally the song ended, and Verona's face was flushed as it beamed up at me. We parted and bowed to each other, my cousin running off as my guests lightly applauded us. Atlas joined in with the ovation, winking as I began to walk towards him. The action brought, in fact, a shy smile to my face that was without a doubt blushing from the extra attention.

I was intercepted, however, by Jacques. At his side were a pleasant woman and, I presumed, her father. He was a tall man, with an austere demeanor similar to my own father. His eyes were dark brown, practically black, and he had an even darker head of hair.

"Young lord, may I introduce Reverend Marquardt," Jacques stated as the both of us gave each other a small bow, "and his daughter, Lady Evelyn." Just barely of-age, the woman's appearance mirrored her father's—pale skin and melancholic features. The pair were clothed in black, though the fabrics were lush and rich still, as they held themselves with poise. Upon their breasts, large ornate crosses glimmered in the afternoon sun.

I had met Reverend Marquardt in passing before, as the Marquardts were a well-known family in the circle of London's supernatural creatures, all of whom were devout patrons to their church. Reverend Marquardt was the choice preacher of the local nobles and common creatures in the area. His sermons were similar to any other preacher's, I supposed—full of fire and brimstone—but his care of his flock's immortal souls was what drew in the practitioners. It was truly a most successful ruse, as they were our first line of defense for all noble families that were of unnatural birth. Being a pillar of piety gave the Marquardt family a status within the community wherein they were able to silence any rumors that arose, true or otherwise, to ensure that no supernatural family would be persecuted.

They were a family of grims. That is, wolf-like creatures that protected the grounds of various church graveyards during the night hours. In other words, the Marquardts were a sort of subspecies of shifter. Though, compared to my own ability to partially and wholly transform my body into that of any animal, they were only capable of transforming into black canines. Many creatures had transformative abilities, also known as an ability to "shift" into a different form. All were answerable to my own family, who was at the helm of the species and were considered most powerful.

Shapeshifters, such as the Avalones, do not have definite life spans. My father—although appearing to be in his late thirties—was many centuries old. This was another contributing factor in our superiority to other creatures that also fell under this blanket term of shifters. The magic in our blood was strong, and from it we harnessed an incredible ability of regeneration. Avalones lived long, seemingly immortal lives, which only could be ended by unsurmountable bodily damage. Disease could not claim us, and we were among only a handful of creatures like this. Beyond that, we were among the only ones which had a decent population, outnumbered only by Vampires.

Grims and others generally labeled as shifters are not like this, although they do live much longer than humans on average and could go on to live quite long lives. Disease could plague them, however, and they would age, albeit at an extremely delayed pace. This was evident on Reverend Marquardt's lined and greying face. All grims will eventually perish and to the earth be returned.

My eyes had drifted back to Atlas during these introductions. He waved a hand to me, signaling that we would catch up later, seemingly drawn into his own conversation with a lass. Reluctantly, my gaze fell back to Lady Marquardt, who although young already possessed a seemingly distant demeanor much like her father. Her hands were folded demurely before her, distant brown eyes gazing at me. I offered my hand to her, and she accepted it. Hers was small and delicate within mine, and I turned it to place a kiss upon it.

"How wonderful to make your acquaintance, Lady Marquardt," I offered these words to the grim, formal as all introductions to another should be, but lacking in sincerity.

"Evelyn if you would please, my lord," her own response mirrored mine. We both were aware that our meeting was simply one of business. She dipped into a curtsy as my lips parted from her hand, her brown eyes gazing up at me as she rose. "Would I be allowed a dance, my lord?"

"Thaddeus, if you please," I corrected, preferring my own name to titles. A more relaxed smile came to her features, and with our hands clasped together we walked out onto the floor. We kept appropriate space between us as we sauntered to the music.

"It would seem that our fathers are interested in us being wed to one another," her sweet voice whispered, the conversation thus remaining intimately between us.

"So it would seem. I frankly have very little knowledge in the matter and assume I will be told when others deem it time." My statement received a small laugh, Evelyn nodding her head in agreement to what I said.

"'Tis our curse," she stated, "to be simply pawns for our parents to use to negotiate the best deal for themselves." She sighed, giving a small twirl under my arm before returning.

"A curse is a good way to describe it," I replied, offering a sincere affirmation to her. During this exchange, I caught sight of my father standing beside Reverend Marquardt. The pair engaged in conversation, no doubt negotiating us away. I gave a low chuckle, effortlessly spinning us. "Even now, they are discussing who will gain more lands from this deal, as if we are chattel," I cynically stated.

Her own reserved eyes glanced at the men, and she let out a short breath. "It would appear to be that way," she stated flatly. I recognized this air of defeat about her, for it was the same helplessness I often felt. My fate was not my own and would be deemed regardless of my wishes, as definitive decisions were chosen by someone else.

"Well, nothing is going to stop us from our own negotiation, wouldn't you say?" I offered. Truth was that I could not offer lands—as they were not mine—nor jewelry or anything of value, but I could offer what our life together would entail. She raised a brow, curiosity sparked in her dour eyes as she nodded in approval for me to continue. "I can offer to be kind, speak to you the truth as I know it to be, and let you choose how the house is decorated in its entirety."

The woman blinked at me, her cheeks brightening in color as she began to titter. "That is quite a generous bargain you offer me, Thaddeus." Her expression mellowed, and her cold, icy exterior melted as we grew comfortable with one another. She twirled under my arm once more. "Well, I can assuredly offer to you my loyalty, politically speaking...As well as a tightly household run. Everything will be as presentable as our houses are expected to be. The terms you have offered and what I, as well, propose are conditions I would be able to accept moving forward," she stated as the pair of us continued our caper.

I nodded to Evelyn, "I find these terms quite agreeable myself." The song faded, and I stepped back, with the woman's small hand still in my own as I bowed to her. Lady Marquardt, in return, curtsied low.

I held her hand up to breast level as we walked back to our fathers, who were still engaged in conversation. I bowed to Lady Marquardt once more, and she offered a curtsy, before she settled next to her father's side again. My own sire chuckled at his continued conversation with the reverend grim, paying me no mind.

"What we must determine, Walter, are some of the finer details, such as where they will reside, as well as the allowance you will provide," my father continued his negotiation of my marriage.

The conversation merely consisted of trivial matters, and my attention wandered. I was not yet dismissed and as such could not leave the conversation, but Jacques could assuredly inform me of anything noteworthy later. I scanned the conversing guests, my eyes searching for Atlas, longingly seeking out his head of curly blonde hair. My search, however, was fruitless, as I was unable to identify him among the surrounding guests. The realization caused a heavy weight to resume its perch upon my shoulders and in my heart. A hollow pit within my stomach made its presence known.

A clearing of someone's throat—Jacques, most likely—brought my attention back to the conversation and dealing away of my life.

"It would, of course, be expected for your son to take Evelyn to mass every Sunday and to the numerous sacrosanct activities she is involved in," Reverend Marquardt stated.

"Of course, that would not be a problem," my father stated, waving his hand. "Another ear providing a line of defense to the nobles is what he will be for us, freeing up yourself to turn your attention to other matters." My father took a sip of his chalice, inspection falling to Evelyn. To her credit, she did not flinch nor look away, and she did so without difficulty. "If I may ask, Walter, I never met your late wife. What was her marker?"

The reverend sighed, "My wife was a beta, and Evelyn is as well."

His chest rose as he made a small *harrumph* noise. "Although, both possess obedience similar to that which any omega might have," he added on.

That piqued my interest for a moment. Interesting was the fact that my father would consider a mere beta as a wife for me. After all, he was an individual who cared deeply about titles and appearances. While I did not discriminate against one marker over another, I knew my father was someone who did, though I was not left to wonder long as to his reasoning.

"A beta is ideal," my father was quick to state, "as I have no intention of stepping down from the head of our family. I would not appreciate any more alphas who could challenge my position." I could feel my father's gelid gaze shift onto me, and despite the rising instinct to lower my head, I kept it high.

His stare was short-lived, falling from me back to the reverend, and he said, "A second generation beta will likely result in any offspring with the same marking, which is very ideal indeed." My father plotted, a satisfied grin coming to his lips. "I think if you are in agreement with me, Walter, we should go and officially draw up the paperwork for this marriage," my father suggested, setting his glass to the side, hands clasping behind his back as he walked away. With another *harrumph* the reverend left us too, hurriedly scuttling after him.

With their departure, the realization that my fate had been decided—without any of my own input, as quick and simple as purchasing clothes—fell upon me. I could feel myself blankly staring, trying to remember how to breathe. The music was suddenly too loud, and the guests were too many. Faintly, I could hear Lady Marquardt speaking and realized my eyes had fallen to the ground, for now I sluggishly looked up at her.

I vaguely realized that her expression mirrored mine. It was sheer disbelief that her persons had been sold away before her eyes. She was offering me words of comfort, or perhaps demands, but though her mouth moved, her voice was drowned out by the roaring sound of my heart hammering in my ears. I turned from her and felt a hand fall on my shoulder. I knew it to be Jacques, likely urging me to listen to my bride-to-be and remember the etiquette expected of me.

"Do not touch me!" I hissed, hitting his hand that had reached out to me.

Though he would offer me solace—and wise words too, no doubt—I could not listen to them now. I walked away from them, tightness gripping at my chest, stealing the air from my very lungs. If either Lady Marquardt or Jacques called after me, I could not know, as the sound of blood rushing consumed whatever I heard. I turned from the party, heading towards the hedge maze on a farther part of the property. My skin was burning, the ring on my finger feeling ice cold as its magic fought to maintain my mundane appearance.

The maze itself was something I had memorized in my youth, and even in this state of distress, I easily strode through its many paths, heading for its far east corner. There were four exits or entrances to this maze, each with their own fountains of magnificent beauty. The farthest, however, was the most precious to me. A wedding gift to my father and mother, this fountain was the first placed in these hedges. The fountain figure was modeled after my mother, draped in loose fabrics and appearing soft, like a goddess of Greek mythology. Rose bushes were planted here and wildly grew. Aside from myself, I do not believe anyone visited this corner of the estate, and thus it was overgrown. But at least it was my own.

Small lanterns illuminated its paths, giving the maze an ethereal glow in the dimming day's light—a practically wasted effort, as not a soul but my own would likely tread through these passages. My hand clutched my chest, still trying to breathe. Being the only individual in this labyrinth, I was able to find the desired solitude and finally began to breathe easier. Though my bones still ached, my skin no longer seemed to be crawling, and the impulse to shift faltered. Finally, I took in a deep breath, lips quivering as I tried to exhale.

I had known that this day would come. Nothing leading up to this foretold stripping of my own decisions had given me hope to believe otherwise. Yet, persisting was a small flame, a flicker of thought that I could have any say or decision. Instead, I was met with this foreseeable outcome. Despite my better judgement, I still was crushed and disgusted with the only path forward.

Reaching this secluded section of the gardens, I paused upon its threshold. I was *not* alone. Perched at the fountain was the human who had captured my attention earlier in the evening. In the dull lantern light, his golden locks seemed to catch every fraction of its glow. He quietly studied the evening sky, oblivious to my presence. This day had been full of emotional extremes, my mental state rampantly rotating between these high and low antipodes.

All at once, I realized the true source of my despair—unaware, he stood before me. Our worlds were completely opposite, and that polarity drew me to him. The man was fetching and masculine, but he possessed hints of femininity that drew me in. Yet, it was also our ease of conversation, how neither of our titles mattered and all else melted away. Together, we had simply held a conversation and found laughter and enjoyment from it.

A tear fell upon my check as the humors of the day finally

gripped my heart in an unimaginably bitter vise. I nearly felt I would collapse as this torrent overwhelmed me. I reached a shaking hand out, rustling the hedges when I searched for hold to steady myself. His hair bounced as he turned in my direction, a bright smile illuminating his face.

"Oh, hello," his voice was full of mirth as a compassionate grin spread across his face.

His lips did turn down then, concern written upon his face at my state. He was quick to stand, hurrying to my side. In response, I swiftly turned away, hand covering my face from his view. The emotions that bubbled up within my chest were conflicting and raw. Anger, shame, fear, anxiety and affection all clawed within me, carving me hollow. The desire to flee from this human—who created such dissension to my very core—surged. Yet as he drew closer, my feet were rooted to the ground, incapable of retreating. It was a force greater than myself, securing me to my post. Atlas stood before me, his beautiful blue eyes gazing up at me, yearning to know the source of my anguish.

"Thaddeus, what has happened?" he asked tenderly.

His pliant hands reached up to my face, but my arm was swift to grab his shoulder, trying to hold him at bay. Gods above, how I was torn. I wished for him to touch me, and yet not to. The human delicately wrapped his hands around my outstretched and stiffened arm, nuzzling his face against the harsh fist that wrinkled his collar.

"Thaddeus," he gingerly spoke my name, just my name. Yet, the way he spoke encouraged me to relax, to let him come closer.

My strength faltered, and as my arm bowed, the human stepped forward. His eyes were genuine and endearing as his gaze searched out mine. My fingers glided down the lapel of his jacket, grasping the fabric closer to his breast, my own eyes falling. I could not look him in the eye, words stalling on my tongue. His hand nestled upon the side of my face, thumb nimbly grazing my cheek. Contrary to my own state, Atlas easily found words that, though simple, were just what I needed to hear in this moment.

"Hey, it's alright now." His voice was delicate, calming as he spoke quietly. "Surely, telling me can only bring a semblance of relief for you, Thaddeus," he assured.

The human was intimately close, his caress tender. I felt myself yearning for more.

"How could I possibly?" I managed to whisper. Seemingly not my own voice, the words came out in a quiver, "How? When I cannot find the words that reflect...everything."

My eyes finally raised to his, locking with the spectacularly radiant blue that gazed back at me. Atlas tilted his head, a charming smile breaking across his face.

"Then one should demonstrate by action," he stated reverently.

My response to what happened next would be less than graceful, as this iridescent being changed my life forever with his simple action.

He slid his hand to the back of my head, sweeping himself forward till our lips met. He was sure in this action, with strength behind it to prevent my first response of flinching away. At the same time, if I had truly fought, I would have had no difficulty in breaking free. His hold, however, was not one to force this affection upon me, but rather, a grasp that allowed the moment to wash over and consume me.

It was not something that took me by surprise—this kiss he seared upon my lips—as his behavior on this day reflected transparently his ample flirtation. What was a surprise, however, was how deeply within the depths of my soul I hungered for more and ravenously kissed his saccharine lips in return. The world would fall away, fears and insecurities alike faded from my thought as the taste of his mouth devoured my every sense.

CHAPTER 4

Throughout my life, I have always found that time could be a silent adversary but also a true friend. This is a concept that differs for someone with an essentially immortal life, as it is not something which I fear as mortals often do. It can seem endless, and moments can crawl or pass by in a blink of the eye. These perceptions are very much the same, yet time cannot seem fleeting to me, as my life ever continues onward. People and the earth can decay, yet I remain hardly eroded.

There were, however, a few times in my life in which time completely stood still. This entity, this elusive construct, could not penetrate or obscure those rare moments. Laws that govern the natural world would all but cease in those moments. Gravity is a force which attracts any body or object towards the center of Earth, or any physical body which has a distinctive mass. For these intangible times, I was that mass, and everything seemed to repel and attract at once.

The first occurrence of this phenomena, this lapse of natural law, was during my youth. Its singular cause was this human. Atlas. Perhaps it was juvenile naivety, but that first kiss was what triggered this effect in the continuum. The world around us had no consequence, freezing around us as our lips found each other's in passionate connection.

This human had me heeled. His hands tenderly held my face as he stole my very breath. Everything about his actions was pleasant and delicate, his lips pliable as he succulently nibbled at my bottom lip. The small action allotted a small inhale, a parting of my lips that the human took full advantage of. His tongue surged forward, victorious as I yielded to his experience and skills. His delicious taste invaded as his tongue massaged my own.

Atlas had me panting before he finally pulled his lips apart from mine. I was nearly delirious chasing after his sweet taste. A small line of saliva connected us till it broke, falling back against my chin. His alluring blue eyes were illuminated in this afternoon light, a delicate blush across his fair features. We both beheld the other, desire plain on both our faces. His burning eyes seemed to shimmer in the light, a small smirk crossing his beautiful face. He leaned back in, though paused as his eyes studied my face, searching for hesitance.

My own face was flustered, eyes heavily lidded with lust as it pumped through my veins, desire written undoubtedly across my features. An ache of need filled me, upheaving a torrent of aspiration to have his lips on mine once more as his face paused so close to mine, yet cavernously away. My hand loosely held the lapel of his vest, while the other hung uselessly at my side. His look remained, and a flicker of realization sparked in my consciousness as I realized he wished for me to be the initiator of this second kiss. My hands both grabbed the front of his vest, surging forward as I claimed another kiss from Atlas.

He let out an amused chuckle at my enthusiasm, but nonetheless matched the heat that our kiss incited. It was during this second kiss that time seemed to begin once more. There was an awareness that minutes were passing as our teeth clicked together, bodies pressing against one another as our osculating continued. I couldn't seem to get enough of his sweet taste, my heart hammering in my chest as I seemed to be suffocating in the most blissful way.

Homosexual had not been a word that was in my repertoire before this night, nor was it a word that could have been used as an adjective for myself. Not that such a sexuality was considered immoral or wrong to my people. Such relations, of course, were not completely unheard of in the supernatural world, and creatures such as myself were part of a caste that allowed for same-sex relationships. On the other hand, what *was* unheard of—at least to me—were relations between a supernatural creature and a human, with the latter unable to conceive. Despite all of this, such concerns were void to me in that moment, as he drowned me with his sinful kisses.

Finally, breathing became a priority again and the spell of our heated kiss was broken, leaving us to gaze into each other's eyes. Between the dimming light and our feverish exploits, the human's cerulean eyes seemed to nearly glow. I became lost in them, panting as I held the back of his head endearingly. Atlas chuckled, delicately holding my own face, his blonde hair wild and disheveled by my hand.

"Have you always had an attraction to men, or am I a special case?" he inquired, grinning. His face was pink with blush, his freckles popping out against his fair skin.

I let out a chuckle of my own, glancing up at him. I was attracted to Atlas, his features handsome and alluring to me. I hadn't necessarily noticed another man in this manner. That is, I hadn't found one of them attractive before meeting Atlas. My hand remained present at the nape of his neck, and my thumb gently teased the small curls of hair there.

"You are the first," I stated.

He confidently smirked, eyes soaking up my bedraggled state. "Oh? You do not have experience then, with men?" the blonde probed.

"To be fair..." I began, and my fingers deftly lifted the blonde's chin, giving him a small kiss upon his freckled nose. "I have no experience with either sex," I chuckled, and Atlas joined along.

"That's alright," the human soothingly spoke, tucking back wayward strands of my hair. "As long as you are diligent, I am more than willing to teach you," the alluring man quipped with a pleased smirk upon his face. His stare was one of admiration, seeming to take in every detail of my face—an expression which mirrored my own.

We simply looked at each other for these few moments, lost in each other's eyes. The adrenaline from our session of indulgence still coursed through our veins, and every small touch was like a thousand little bells all ringing at once. I was content, so much so that I could have hidden away in this remote part of our garden within close proximity of Atlas for an eternity, but the human seemed to have a proper head upon his shoulders. Unlike me, he realized we could not hide out forever.

He sighed, giving the side of my face a tender pat, "Come, surely the host of honor will soon be missed if we dally too long." An easy laugh followed, his eyes unable to turn from my own.

I helped adjust his vest, the perfectly pressed cloth having been disturbed by my hands. I didn't hide the displeasure upon my face of having to return to the party, but dinner was undoubtedly nearing. It was the part of the evening I could not miss, above all else. The more sensible part of me was finally able to break through the torrent of emotions and flare-up of adrenaline, and I knew that I would have to return.

"You are correct," I dryly chuckled and tilted my head down at him, steeling myself to return to the party. He shifted up onto the tips of his toes, stealing one more brief kiss before he sauntered away from me.

"I often am," he called back. The human paused at the corner of the hedge, glancing back at me with a small smile on his lips. "See you at the races, Thaddeus." He winked before disappearing around the edge of the bushes.

I sat by myself for a moment more, an amused little smirk upon my lips at the anticipation of what the next racing events could entail. It wasn't difficult to go face the party once more, as my thoughts were occupied by Atlas alone. I adjusted my attire, giving my trousers a quick dusting off before navigating my way through this labyrinth, back to the party.

My head was spinning from the adrenaline, but slowly it wore off, and the rest of the evening passed with relatively uneventful occurrence in comparison to those previous stolen moments. Dinner was grand and luxurious with bountiful food, though I frankly cannot recall if I ate a single thing. My head was elsewhere, thoughts occupied by Atlas' lips and the mesmerizing picture of his blue eyes. I was present for conversations and other dealings that came with the territory of the evening, but the contents were vacant in me. As my birthday celebration continued well into the evening, the illuminance of candles and lanterns gave an ethereal glow to the gardens. Elite and socially familiar groups became established, surrounding tables as they gambled, conversed business or both.

Respective servants to the lords and ladies stood at attention behind them.

I found myself seated at a more secluded table. Jacques was prompt in directing me toward it upon my emergence from our labyrinth grove, though not without a disapproving glance regarding my evaporation. Lord Marquardt and my father were seated at their own table, discussing amongst themselves what I could only assume were strategic plans for the continued concealment of the supernatural populace in London. At the table closest to my own, Lady Marquardt sat alone, her own servant standing at attention behind her. Without much expression, she observed others, sitting ramrod straight in her chair. A cup of tea was present on the table before her but sat seemingly untouched.

Upon my approach to the table she rose, and as proper etiquette dictated, she lowered into a curtsy. She straightened and her brown eyes landed on me as I, too, mirrored her action. Then, the both of us sat down at the table, not quite sure what to say to one another. Lady Marquardt was the first to find her voice.

"Your father and my own plan to announce our engagement before the end of summer, though it seems for the moment that they have yet to set a date for us." Her voice was dry as she looked out onto the party. She seemed almost as distraught about our situation as I was. Through my Atlas-addled brain, I recalled my behavior and knew I had acted unsavorily.

"Evelyn," I began, her attention back to me as I spoke her name. "I apologize for my behavior before, but I needed to clear my head."

She was generous and smiled at me, although I could see that she was every bit as terrified as I was to have no control over these important decisions. I reached out a hand, and the female beast before me looked so lonely and scared, though she did well to hide it. If it were not for the fact that I felt the same things myself, I may not have noticed, but her feelings were a mirror of my own.

I exhaled, continuing, "It is not every day that one of the most important decisions of my life is ripped from my own choosing, but..." My hand kindly held hers, and I made sure to have my eyes meeting hers as I spoke, "To you I swear, while we may be forced into this match, I will do my best to be kind and courteous to you in our lives together, but above all..."

I paused, for even the words I spoke now could be a lie to her. Betrothed for all intents and purposes, my mind instead lingered away, yearning for the lips of a human I had just met. To that point, I was infatuated with a male, incapable of bearing children. Though I could have been construed as many things during my life, I never intended to be a liar. Thus, with complete authenticity I spoke the following words to her.

"Above all, Evelyn, I will never force upon you a decision that is mine to make. Nor, time permitting—if you will so bless me with them—will I allow such a burden as we here face to befall our children." I sincerely spoke to Evelyn, knowing that this promise I could in fact keep and uphold for her.

The female's eyes shimmered, for the moment accepting all that I could offer in this situation. She looked away, blinking to clear her eyes, doing as best as she could to hide how she truly was still scared, but my words were a comfort, nonetheless. She gave my hand a squeeze, a smile of appreciation present upon her face.

Our fathers had concluded their conversation, and the reverend stood, expressing his farewells. Evelyn and I stood as well, myself bowing to her, and from her a curtsy—acts we could look forward to in excess. I took her hand and modestly kissed it.

"Till our next meeting, miss," I stated.

She returned the statement with another smile, falling to her father's side as they retired from the evening. I was the same, holding my head high, hands clasped behind the small of my back. My father remained stoic for a moment or two, watching my father-in-law and bride-to-be withdrawing from the gardens. During this moment, I observed that his cheeks had the faintest hint of color to them—misplaced, given that he rarely had such a complexion. I quickly surmised that it was brought on from spending the afternoon and evening drinking.

I could not leave without my father's dismissal, and finally he gave a small nod, a low huff from his chest. "This is good, indeed," he remarked, a dark plotting smirk on his lips.

My father turned from me and walked away. His words left me with a lingering sense of trepidation—something that in the moment I did not heed but would understand all too well in time.

CHAPTER 5

Rumors and gossip among the elite of society were the pinnacle of activities with which to fill one's day. Words traveled seemingly upon the wind, with feet nimbler than any beast as they jumped from host to host. The contents, regardless of accuracy, were always coveted for one's own collection. The status of my engagement breathed to life like wildfire, with circles of both supernatural and mundane groups alike devouring every detail of the situation.

For the mundane, curiosity was centered around why an obviously devoted patron of the church was to be my bride, rather than their own daughters, for those families had much more power and influence in their eyes. Harsher still, the Lady Marquardt—although betrothed to me—still faced heated competitors, who thought themselves more worthy to be in her position. From this cluster sprouted the seeds of hearsay regarding her legitimacy, beauty, health and virginal status.

As for the families who either were supernatural or had ties to families that were, they too conversed falsities. Their criticisms, though, were not a reflection of their 'unchosen' status. All knew that this match was conceived, above all, for the continued concealment of supernatural families. This match provided an easier thread of communication between those amongst the sheep—that is, the Marquardt Family and the Avalones, who funded this shroud. The families who knew what we were and what kind of person Cenric Avalone was would never want their daughters to be married into such a family. The most recent example of being married into the Avalone family was my mother—and her people's disposal once their purpose had been served was well-known.

There was, of course, the situation of the archaic caste system that still held powerful influence among the supernatural families, to which the Avalone family was no exception. The majority of supernatural creatures (especially so during the 1700s) had an additional marker of hierarchy in reference to their persons. Whereas most all creatures will be born biologically male or female—this is the *primary sex*—the supernatural individual will also possess an additional *secondary sex*. This is often referred to as a *marker* in conversation, and it is generally determinable once the onset of puberty begins. Of these secondary sexes there are three: alpha, beta and omega. Physically, this can make the body appear differently than the traditional male or female body, as perceived by humans. These differences are more of a case-by-case resolution, and even humans can fall into this caste, being deemed as betas.

Traditional families believe that the alpha is to lead, betas are meant to follow and omegas are to be their servants, as the alpha deems fit. Nowhere was this belief more absolutely upheld than in my own family. My father had been *the* alpha in our family for many years and clutched the title closely. Such a title as his allowed him sole authority on behalf of the family and, per the structure of jurisdiction at the time, for the whole of supernatural families within Great Britain's borders and her reach. I am the sole heir to my father, and as the only alpha left to claim such a title, my potential offspring and I have always been a threat to him. Thus has been the case ever since I first presented as an alpha. Such as the situation is, many speculate and whisper about what shall happen should the Marquardts displease the reigning alpha.

Another topic of gossip was the actual matter of my match. Many creatures have the capability of shifting to a different skin, though typically only between two forms. A more humanistic appearance is often accompanied by magic trinkets, to conceal a beast's true form. Perhaps the best example of this can be described in the case of werebeasts, a category which my betrothed Evelyn was a part of. She could appear human, but her beast form was that of a large black canine. My own family views themselves as an elite form of this race, as they can shift into a collection of a few creatures.

Another reason for this mindset is that shapeshifters such as my kind have difficulty crossbreeding. With another shapeshifter, a resulting pregnancy is highly likely to occur. With a werebeast, however, the birth rates plummet—though a small percentage of possibility remains that a child could be conceived. A delicate balance of conditions must be met, including the female being in heat or a heavily fertile period of time during a breeding season. In addition, the pair has to be genetically compatible to produce children. For creatures outside of these groups, the possibility of conception is nonexistent. Thusly, in the days following the party and the public announcement of our engagement, many people including myself were left to wonder.

Why would my father choose someone who could *potentially* provide me with an heir, someone to further challenge his own position if born an alpha? Superstition surrounds statistics regarding the genetic circumstances that determine an individual's marker. One instance of such an opinion is that a child conceived from a pairing involving a beta—as either the mother or sire—often results in that child being beta themselves. However, I have observed that it can be merely a roll of the dice. One must keep in mind that during this time, the Punnett square had not yet been discovered.

My father could have very easily chosen a family wherein the production of an offspring was impossible—the women for this potential were nearly endless. Yet, the alpha of Great Britain had chosen a werebeast, with whom I would have at least a chance of conceiving an Avalone heir. The magnitude of speculation on the decision of my betrothal provided a bountiful source of conversation, guesses ranging from supposition that the Lady Marquardt was infertile, to her family not being the creatures they claimed to be. Some even speculated that my father lusted to use her as his own.

Though I myself detest such poisonous conversations that these rumors produce, it is always better to be in the know of what is spoken about you. For that, Jacques provides my greatest asset. Though more geared toward his role as my own retainer, Jacques is also head of the household, in terms of rank among the servants. The head butler and housekeeper answer to him or my father's own personal footman. As such, when a particularly poignant suggestion comes to the household's radar, Jacques is among the first to know. When it concerns me, I am then the next. It was from him that I heard this list of rumors.

It was another cool morning, a few weeks after the announcement had been made public. Having no immediate plans for the morning, I had taken breakfast in bed. Jacques stood at the foot of the bed, having relayed these whispers and gossip with a quite sour expression. The statements troubled me, out of respect for Lady Marquardt. She was, above all, a pious woman and had been thrown into this situation just as I had.

I looked up from my meal and asked, "What would your opinion be moving forward, Jacques?"

The truth of the matter was that his insights would always weigh more than my own. Jacques had seen his own many honest years, being in the service of my parents long before my birth. As it was just us in the room, Jacques was more relaxed, his hands resting at the small of his back. He walked to a window, gazing out upon London as he thought on the matter.

"Well, sir, I am left to wonder how Lady Marquardt feels on the matter. She is not in a position to defend herself, for the ridiculous reason of her womanhood. If your intentions are in fact true, as well as your promise to her, I would act in such a way that does defend her."

This man often could be straight and to the point, but whenever I desired a straightforward answer, he would be aloof and almost mystical in his responses. Today seemed to be one of those such occasions.

Though my heart was troubled by these vile rumors, my social movements were quite limited, in fact. Such was my life, and to call upon Lady Marquardt would undoubtedly present its own challenges from her family. With the talk of scandal already abundant, further rumors must be prevented at all costs. The both of us had been left isolated by the announcement and subsequent intrigue of our pairing, and I could only imagine Lady Marquardt's own inner turmoil while having to remain pure and pious through this challenge.

I sighed, pinching the bridge of my nose between my thumb

and index finger. Though the matter of my betrothal was a very real and raw reality of my situation, simultaneously remaining in my mind was the thought of the human who had charmed me so. My thoughts often dwelled on the mundane being, my heart aflutter, thinking upon when we could next meet. An idea sparked, my head quickly lifting as I looked at Jacques.

"Surely a gesture on my part is in order. Word must be sent to Lady Marquardt inviting her to the races...and to bring a lady along with her for feminine company." I paused but followed this idea with, "For my company, I would as well like to invite Lord Atlas Charron. With all of us in the same age group, surely an outing would be allowed by all houses involved." I speculated, then added on, "Two sections—one for the ladies and one for the gentlemen—at the Avalone estate's expense."

My instructions brought a glimmer to Jacques' eyes, a proud expression brought on by my decision, and he took his leave to do as instructed.

Perhaps getting away from our households would be a good thing, although my motives for the orchestration of such an outing were, admittedly, not wholly to help the image of my engagement to Evelyn. It undoubtedly would do so, but my truest reason was to see the human once again. He occupied my every wandering thought. *Why* was something I could not deduce. Maybe because it was forbidden, but I never had coveted another for simple carnal pleasure. His whole being drew me in—his smile and the light in his eyes, his underutilized charismatics were my ultimate weakness. I desired to spend long hours with him, to know why my attraction and desire were so rampant.

A frustrated groan left me as I pressed the palms of my hands to my face. My soul's inner turmoil already had me exhausted, de-

spite the early hour. This was a wretched position I was in, yearning for what I knew deep down I could not have. All the same, my
desire remained. In doing so, these desires made me unfaithful and
duplicitous towards Evelyn. This situation created a heavy-hearted
ache, the struggle of my desires and duty pitted against the other.
This internal battle indeed had its claws deep in me, and the despair
was a constant, looming presence.

The only consolation I pined for was the possibility that although this marriage was inevitable, I could allow freedom some-
day—when perhaps we were not as entrapped in the clutches of our
households. Over time, Evelyn and I could cultivate a fondness for
one another, but I could never expect her to love me, nor would
I require any more affection from her than a public image. This
maintenance of public perception was something I had no desire
for, but nonetheless, it was of the utmost expectancy for our clans
and was truly the reason for contentment in our pairing. Such a
position—though I was alone in this knowledge—was what could
help to tame the despair I harbored and provided enough comfort
that I was able to get myself out of bed each morning.

On this morning in particular, I simply threw on a robe and
decided to take up residence in my study. In the life of a young supernatural lord, hours of the day and night were heavily devoted
to studying. Understanding the secrets of our community and the
controlled story that mundanes were fed was of utmost importance.
Still yet, there was old magic that lay asleep in this world, constantly
monitored for rumors of it being awakened, so that in such a case it
could be hastily dealt with, thus concealing our presence.

Books and ancient texts of lore were spread across my desk, as
well as my own notes and sketches chaotically organized around
my study. The topic I was immersed in: omnipotent creatures

known. Gods, to be more precise, which was a title given and observed by mundanes solely. Among supernatural beings like myself, such creatures were simply viewed as leaders, true alphas, and the original beings of their race in our world. Their presence was scarce.

Dragons particularly had drawn my interest—their rarity unparalleled, such that even in my secluded world the truth of their existence remained curiously but a legend. They were rumored to possess strength and magical abilities at a tier that sat equal with angels and high demons. All information known was archaic, the presence and numbers unknown. The document I was pouring over—my work at translating a primitive text—appeared to be one of many creation stories, something which I found most fascinating. Reading these texts brought a fond smile to my face, as the particular story I was deciphering held much resemblance to a bedtime story my mother used to tell me. Her people's beliefs vastly differed from my sire's land, and it was her narrating voice ringing in my head.

The universe had but two elements, of two opposite households from which all creatures come: the darkness of the world and the light. Each had their army, with loyalty driven into each and every general's core. The wars were fought daily, but without casualty, and this dance continued for millennia.

Among these generals of the light was the most beautiful creature. Her hair was fair, so blinding that none could look upon it directly. She was the oldest of light, porcelain yet strong. For her beauty and kindness, smarts and valor, she ranked highest among the generals of the light. Even so, she grew weary of the war. Nothing but this war was what she had known, and though loyal to her party's plight, she yearned for something more.

During one battle, she came across something so different and surprising that she halted her advance to observe. It was then, for the first time in millennia, that the battle had ceased. Both sides were perplexed, gazing in wonder. Something had appeared but was so foreign to the generals, who had known either the light or the dark and nothing more. What had appeared was water and earth. It was fascinating, it was new, it was something different!

The fairest maiden of light was the first to touch these things. The earth was soft—something you could stand upon, it was sturdy yet uneven. Where her bare feet stepped, she left marks upon this earth, and upon her soles the same. Next, she observed water. Stepping into it and saturating her feet, it was cool to the touch, and she found that funny. Submersing herself made her feel weightless, supported by this thing she had found. All the generals then played, taking joy in these new things that had appeared. The maiden was, however, the most curious. She wanted to see what would happen if these two fantastic things—earth and water—were combined. A handful of generals from both sides did the same, combining these two things to see what would happen.

It was the fairest maiden general of the light who created first, though. She continued to combine and made sculptures from the mud, and each general (no matter belonging to the dark or light) followed suit. The fairest maiden toiled and formed the most magnificent sculptures. In total, there were four. She was proud of her creations, and all the generals gazed in wonder. However, when the waters rose, they disappeared—nothing left but piles of mud, and all mourned. This made the maiden and all the generals, despite being light or dark, wail in despair.

The maiden loved her creations, and in her melancholy, she did the most unlikely and wondrous thing. As she wept, tears fell from her beautiful face. She held her creations close and gave to each a kiss. This was the first use of magic, for the love she bore for her creations was so strong that she became the first creator. The sculptures began to move as she breathed life into them, and all stared in wonder. Both houses alike, those of light and those of dark, swelled in song and chanted her name, "Mother! The greatest creator! The first creator!"

These four creatures were the first. Translated to the modern tongue, they are called the four cardinal dragons. In them were the powers of the winds, and with each movement as they came further to life, great joy was given to all who bore witness. From that day forth, many generals became creators, creating the gods and their kin and all manner of beasts and things.

Mother, the most beautiful general of light, would be the one alone who could give life to the creations. Though they were molded by many, only her tears—wept in anguish at their possible loss—and a farewell kiss brought them life. Thereafter, many beautiful and wonderful things came about. Vegetation and mountain ranges were born, as well as the life therein. Even when brought by creatures of the dark, she wept the same for them and thus breathed life into each and every being.

Soon the world became a place, crawling with inhabitants and the little gods, who then began to make their own creations. The mother breathed life into many, but her first children were the first dragons. The four cardinal directions were known, and to each their own power was bestowed, which helped in shaping this world.

First were the twins, the alphas of the dragons. Their winds were of the East and South. The eastern wind, Küiki, was as fair as her mother. She was the strongest with control of her winds, her mind sharp and invading. Her power was in the great ocean storms and coastal breeze. The southern wind was Ke'ahi. His strength was in the wind of fires, for consuming and omnipotent was his power. His destruction is seen where wildfires claim and ravage the landscapes. Third was the beta, the wind from the West. Tälamh was his name. He was calmer and the most calculative of his siblings. The power of his winds was seen in the eruption of volcanoes or the earth quaking beneath. Finally, was Câlder. He was the omega and wind of the North. Cold and secluded, he was fair and beautiful, but not more so than his sister or mother. His power is seen in the great storms of winter and the death they bring.

Dragons were the first created and shall be the last to perish. Proud of her children—those of darkness or light or of something between—the mother held claim of all. The war had ended, and the generals fell asleep. Time was now for the gods to create.

This translation was one version of the oldest and truest bedtime story that all supernatural children were told about how we came into creation. This was the version my mother had told me, and coming across it did bring a small smile to my face. I set the document aside and settled back in my chair, mulling the words over. This story sprung many legends and fundamentally understood concepts or reasoning behind each species. Humans do not understand as we do, that there was not one true god in any sense. Many were created, and thus all were valid. What merely mattered was where one's allegiance lay, and thus would be one's fate both in life and—where appropriate—thereafter.

I crossed my arms, closing my eyes as I pondered this matter, the bout of nostalgia running rampant through my mind. The purpose of such research that I and many other young lords and ladies were tasked with was to find either a weapon or spell that could combat such despotic beings. As it was now, many of the creations which were elemental or godly—such as the first dragons—were asleep. Long ago, in fact, had they fallen asleep, and the location of their crypts was forgotten. It is worth mentioning here that the most common beasts to rouse and pillage, or at the very least cause hysteria in wake, were dragons. Not the original four mind you, at least not yet. That being said, no one had seen or known of a dragon since medieval times. Considering how well my family blended with humanity, however, it would not be unthinkable that they might be hidden in plain sight as well.

More often than not, this weapon was prophesied and pronounced in all religions in the tale of an imminent apocalypse. Looking back to old Norse tales depicting Ragnarök or more recent religions foretelling impending doomsdays, humans have a tendency to interpret such that the end of life itself is coming. Supernaturals are aware that the case is more likely to be that one of these ancient behemoth gods might awaken to do as they did in ancient times. That is, to create. To much smaller and weaker beings, this could be construed as destruction and an end, though such a great being would not think so.

My contemplation on the subject matter was interrupted by a faint knock, the all too familiar sound of Jacques' hand against the wood. Glancing out the window, I noted that a few hours had passed, for the sun was approaching its midday fixture. Undoubtedly, he brought news of my invitations to the races.

"Enter," I called out, jotting down a note in my ever-lengthening list of thoughts on this task of mine.

Jacques entered the room, a small disapproving sigh passing his lips at my lazing state of attire. I took no notice, as often I had witnessed this look of his, and almost always it was cast in my direction. He folded his hands at the small of his back, giving a small nod and smile upon speaking.

"Word has been sent from the Marquardt family. They have permitted allowance of this outing with Lady Evelyn back to your lordship. Such as prescribed, that the lady will be sat with a maiden for company and your lordship with his own companion. Conversational distance must be observed in such a way that no foul play has purpose to sprout among those who speak heresy of the Lady Marquardt."

He stated this news with a small glint in his eye, a look urging me to follow these terms exactly. A nod confirmed my compliance.

I was grateful for this chance to squash rumors of the wicked tongued. Evelyn without doubt was the same as I—thrown into such a situation with little control. Despite the fact that it was so, her character proved and remained pure. She was dedicated to remaining an exemplary bride-to-be. I had every intent to show the same compliance and to make this situation easier with my actions. Though my heart fluttered for another reason.

I rose from my chair as I spoke, "And for Lord Atlas? What was his reply?"

The twinkle in Jacques' eye remained, and a smile finally broke across his aged face after a momentary, yet eternal pause. One small nod confirmed Atlas' attendance, and my heart sang.

CHAPTER 6

I had received a unanimous and resounding acceptance to my invitation, leaving me in a state of mirth. In the days that followed, I ordered for the arrangements to be made while excitement and anticipation bubbled in my chest. I was not as devoted to my tasked studies and research. Instead, I took long walks around the estate with my own eager thoughts and daydreams for company. As often was the case in this place, however, any emotion resembling happiness was short-lived.

In the early morning hours, barely minutes into what would be a new day, word was passed to wake me. This was a difficult task, as I was a creature who slept quite soundly in my youth—not to mention the additional hold of dreams burying my consciousness. My dreams often were a manifestation of the fantastical works or legends I read during the daytime hours and created a safe plane of existence to escape. My dreams were a place that, since my meeting of the human Atlas, was instead dominated with his presence.

Some dreams were more tame or domestic in subject matter. The two of us would be entangled in the other's limbs as we cuddled close to one another. Languid and tender kisses traversed over one another's exposed skin. Waking from these dreams, when always I would find myself filled with regret and longing for moments more, I swore I could smell his honey scent present in the room. It was as if he were an incubus that had slipped in unknowingly and actually played out the innocent skits, only to disappear before I could wake and make them a reality.

Other dreams were devoid of such innocence. Heated and hungry visions left my belly and loins burning for release when I would suddenly wake. Dripping in sweat, I would writhe in my bedding, choking back damning moans and pressing my face into my pillows. It was this latter version of dreaming that enriched my sleep tonight.

Our hands slowly explored each other's bodies, my kisses hesitant and naive. The Frenchman's own actions gradually became bolder and finally escalated to scandal. Atlas nibbled and sucked, marking my body as his in a possessive manner known only to my kind. The reality was that a human likely would not act in such a way, but the persona he took in my dreams was insatiable and dominating. Like a page flipped in a book, the circumstances would change. The corners of his lips turned impishly upward, mewling my name and dirtily talking in a manner bordering on sacrilegious. Quicker, our bodies moved together, my own chest tightening as I panted and gasped for breath. White hot pleasure pooled in my lower abdomen as his heat pulsed over my skin like a vise. He pulled me against his body and—

The dream melted away, turning black and vanishing into nothing. I was roused by my shoulder, being grasped and shaken in a not-at-all considerate manner.

"Young lord, you are needed most urgently!" It was Jacques' own tired but pressed voice waking me. Again, he forcefully shook me and hissed, "Further delay will surely not bode well, Thaddeus."

In his other hand he held a candelabra, and my amber eyes slitted in the light. I winced away at first but then rapidly blinked as they adjusted to the light. Groggily coming to, it took a few moments to reach full alertness. Clarity struck me like Thor's hammer, my eyes widening at the presence of another so close—given my vulnerable and sensitive state.

"J-Jacques...what..." I began, though the words trailed off as he turned from me.

He set the candelabra down, holding up a thin robe he had slung over his arm and now urging me to slip it on. Jacques explained, "Your presence has been ordered by your father, who—excuse my blunt use of words—is in quite a foul mood."

The witch's voice was short, and the glow of candlelight cast a veil of dark foreboding upon his face. He wore only his night clothes and his own robe that protected him from the evening chill. His face was taut and haunting, brows pinched together in worry. Knowing that my father's mood would worsen should I dawdle, I did not need to be told twice and rose from the bed. I briskly slipped into the offered robe and adjusted so I appeared decent. Just barely having achieved this, Jacques placed a hand to my back and ushered me forward.

Anxiety caught in my throat, though I did manage to whisper to Jacques as we hurriedly left my rooms, "F-Forgiven...Do you know, what it is he...?"

Knowing my nature and the likely anxiety and questions that mounted within me, Jacques gave a small *harrumph* before swiftly responding, "He has gotten some sour news concerning the current conflict between British and French forces in America. It is quite a costly loss involving the capture of a major...and it would seem your father has financing involved..."

Jacques hardly dared to whisper. My father's hearing was like my own—sharp and sensitive—so if he were to hear our discussion, it would undoubtedly not bode well for me. For, the only times in which I was called into his presence (particularly at such an irregular hour) were not for reasons of good-natured, embracing company.

I had intended to ask further questions, but we were already passing through the halfway point of the estate now due to our hurried steps, and the chance of our conversation being overheard was more likely. Also, the part of the estate my father resided in, I realized, was teeming with life at the moment. A queer sight, as it was the dead of night, but that only meant that the news my father had received must have been horrendous. Messengers and staff shuffled around in the halls, and as we neared his office, we heard voices raised in argument. From under the door, warm candlelight cast ominous pillars of light onto the hallway floor, and I felt my heartbeat quicken with growing anxiety.

Here we would be heard, so Jacques could offer no additional comforting words, as it would only further enrage my father and worsen what was coming. His hand slid to my shoulder though, not caring that any peeking soul could see, and squeezed it. Although unease rose as an invisible sort of burning bile in my throat, his physical contact was a comfort.

We were not left waiting long, for the door to his office was thrown open and slammed against the hall wall. A short, black-haired creature—by its scent some sort of lower demon—scuttled out with my father's voice bellowing after him, "You remind them it was *THEIR* choice, an incompetent human—that *GRANT*—

and if he had used some other strategy or tactic that isn't so god-damn *KNOWN,* we would have control of that damned fort, and he wouldn't be sitting as their fucking *PRISONER* right now!" My father's words were thrown out like scalding water after the small creature, who paid no attention to me in his hurried retreat.

The conflict that was being discussed, though I knew little of it at the time due to my sheltered life, was what would later become known as the French and Indian or Seven Years' War. The particular subject we had walked into—which my father had aggressively and with ferocity discussed—had been the initial failed surge on Fort Duquesne. The early years of this war were not going well for the British, and as an investor, my father's funds were hemorrhaging quicker than the ability to reap rewards. This infuriated him. There is always money to be made in war, but it does not happen as expeditiously when you are on the apparent losing side. The prospect of land gained if successful slowly disappears from one's hand when a fort is not seized with an initial siege, as in this case.

"Send in the pathetic half-breed! I can smell him from here... fucking disgusting..." The 'half-breed' he referred to was me. At the best of times, I was a tolerated presence, and at that, only because half of my blood was from him.

I froze. Jacques' description of 'a foul mood' had been used in an all too giving manner. My father was beside himself in boiling rage, and my hide was going to suffer from it tonight. Jacques had borne witness to this scene too many times in my life. While he held great disdain for it, objection would only worsen what my father doled out, and quite possibly, interference would result in his termination. Therefore, my torment would continue on, regardless. If he were terminated, Jacques could not offer comfort or care in the aftermath. My being truly alone in the face of such parental hatred would be a deadly consequence, so we endured in our own way. Without a word, Jacques' hand squeezed my shoulder once more, reminding me that he was there for me, and I was not alone. He then reluctantly pushed me forward into this wolf's den.

As I moved into the light of the room, my eyes locked onto my father's swelled form behind his desk, and I remained acutely aware of the immediate threat to my persons. My breath caught, as I hardly dared to breathe, for even such a necessary function could further aggravate the situation I entered. Every inch of the room was meticulous and well organized, not a speck of dust settled on any surface due to diligent cleaning. A healthy and bright fire burned in the hearth and was tended to by a maid, a stack of papers having just been tossed in. Including Jacques and myself, there was a total of five beings in the room.

The maid, who was hunched over and tending to the fire, also seemed to be crying. She did so silently of course, as such an audible sound would earn her only the back of a hand from either my father or the other being in the room. Upon our entering, her bright, tear-filled feline eyes turned our way for a fleeting moment. By the swelling bruise on her cheek, I could see that she had already been hit, and I could feel my lip curling in anger at the sight. She was a simple, unnamed member of our staff, and as such her tasks were conducted silently and with obscurity. Hers was a job that rarely ever caused our paths to cross. Tonight, she had seemingly drawn some short straw that she would tend to my father's witching hour needs. Her performance was apparently not to my father's—nor his clerk's—standard, as evidenced by her bruised face.

"Away with you, girl!" the clerk, Ward, ordered.

Much like Jacques was my own magical shadow and informant, for my father, that position belonged to Ward. He was as cold and nightmarish a creature as my father was, a well-made match that at this point was decades strong. He stood at a podium, seemingly taking down the minutes for this meeting. Dressed properly in iron-pressed attire, this picture along with the dark circles under his eyes gave the impression that he had not even gone to bed yet. This sight was not strange to me. Often the mage appeared as such, and I had concluded in reasoning that evil beings—and I suspect he was one—did not sleep. For that was an indulgent and peaceful thing, and such creatures that thrived on torment and pain could not tolerate more than what was necessary to maintain one's health.

At his word, the girl gathered her skirts, stood, then bowed to the room's inhabitants before darting out. I dared not offer her a look of sympathy as she passed me by, for it very well could recall her to this room of punishment. Still, my heart did ache for her and the treatment she had received. Instead, so as not to give into the temptation of my gentle heart, my glowing amber eyes returned to my father and despite knowing better, I sized him up. He sat at his desk and returned my regard with a glare full of disgust.

Like everyone, excluding Ward, he was in barely more than his sleeping clothes. The news of the failed raid had only reached his bedside presumably in the recent hours. The state of him was a picture I had rarely seen, however, as he did not wear his own magic ring. So he sat before me as he naturally was, and I could compare the vile similarities and unique differences we shared. Whereas I changed quite drastically when not focused on my appearance or not wearing Garmr, my father was not the same. His natural state was quite similar to his edited one and needed little adjustment. The generally accepted reason for this was that after generations of suppressing their state of homeostasis and dealing with persecution, the Old-World shifters evolved to appear more mundane.

My father had short black hair, often brushed back and polished in product, but tonight it was instead loosely swept to the side. A few strands fell against his brow, and in this moment, I realized he possessed more grey hair than the coal black I had always known. He also had heavy facial hair shadowing his chin and above his upper lip. Despite being up at such an odd hour, it was much too early to have shaved. In the current moment, he also did not have a tail present—something which I could not achieve unless helped by Garmr's magic. In the absence of extreme emotion, my sire's family did not bear tails, and this too was a feat they attributed to their superiority. For, they could live in obscurity with ease and thus were more evolved.

Finally, his nearly black eyes were similar to that of a bear which, unlike my own eyes or any other shifter-type creature's, did not faintly glow. They were cold—one would almost say without a soul—but there was a soul present, only it was repugnant and unfeeling. That is, unfeeling spare the burning abhorrence harbored for my presence.

We both had a slight point to our ears. It was the same as with his missing tail, which would not take the shape of a particular animal unless experiencing extreme emotion. This slight point was a tell-tale sign to humans and their lot that we were not of their stalk. Our ears and teeth were the first giveaways to what we were, the latter sharp and inhuman. My own were similar to what my mother's had been, and that meant they were more canine in nature—with four incisors and then a set of interlocking top and bottom canines.

Contrastingly, my father's teeth—much like his icy, dim eyes—resembled those of a bear. Just looking at the upper jaw, he had six incisors, the farthest on either side slightly larger and more pointed, but no more than the two adjacent bulging canines. One of which—the lower left—had broken off quite a long time ago now. This prevented his jaw from tightly closing, so his lip hung down slightly on that side. Even while he grinned maliciously, as he did now towards me, his teeth sat at this awkward angle.

"There is my bastard offspring..."

CHAPTER 7

At the use of such a term—if it were not for the paralyzing fear and anxiety I possessed at the moment—I could have laughed right in his face. It was among his favorite of titles to insult me with, and thus not very original. Yes, often he referred to me as the *bastard offspring* despite my conception and birth all having taken place after he married my mother—a marriage which, by mundane law, had been sound and true, witnessed by the nearly half of London in attendance. I supposed for most of my life this was why he could not get rid of me—the fact that contrary to his jabs of my bastardization, I was his sole heir.

Nevertheless, he hated me, a simple and plain fact I knew and accepted long ago. In such a situation, one must reach acceptance, for the damage of trying to fantasize otherwise would break one's spirit down and collapse the mind. That was a satisfaction I would not allow him, bearing witness to me bound and gagged, carted off to Bedlam.

Our eyes locked again—my own faintly glowing, his frozen and calculating. Our every interaction was like an intense match of chess. Each word or action caused millions of routes that ultimately would result in one of two outcomes. A nagging thought emerged, as it often did before our matches, and I wondered if this time he would take it too far and kill me. It was a very morose and numb thought, but one that surfaced whenever I was trapped like this.

My father's go-to opening move was an insult thrown in my face, and he would then wait for a response. I cannot honestly say whether a response or silence made things worse generally, for each night was different. Tonight in particular, he was very hard to read, but I could recognize his anger. In his brooding glance, I also saw a glint of intended malice, and that meant the match was already set. He was the cat, vicious and ready to strike. I was to be the mouse.

"Good evening, father," I quietly greeted. There was no warmth in my words, and I only returned the cool tone offered to me. Even so, with blinding speed he picked up a paper weight from his desk and threw it at me, catching my right brow and splitting it open.

"I gave you no permission to speak, you filthy half-breed!" He snarled with the ferocity of a bear, his bark rattling the window-panes.

I could feel as blood slipped down my face from the wound, but I dared not to cradle it. Doing so would only make my situation worse, which would be futile. For even before the few exposed drops of blood could hit my shoulder, the wound had begun to close. Another snarl ripped past his lips at this, as if I had consciously healed myself with such speed in defiance.

Shifters in general had fast-acting metabolisms. Despite their large consumption of foods, due to the nobles' diet being rich in proteins and fat, most retained very slender and agile frames. I, myself, was an example of the typical build. Alternately, my father carried much more muscle and weight around his belly than I did, which served as evidence of his gorging and plentiful diet. With such a metabolism, an accelerated healing factor was often the case as well. Here though, I was an anomaly, and it just provided another reason for my father's hatred.

For example and comparison, imagine it were my father or a human who had just taken a paper weight to the face. At the speed it cracked against my skull, it very well could have killed a human, though would not have done so to him. Instead, the large head wound would bleed protrusively, scab over, bruise and leave a scar splitting his brow within a few days.

In my case, given that I was generally well-fed and thus in good health, the item which caused my wound hardly had stopped bouncing to the floor, and I was already healed. Large damage, such as a dislocation or break, would need to be set properly. The healing factor I possessed worked quite quickly, and in this most recent example would heal before the end of the day. If it were a more serious injury and had not been set properly, it would heal incorrectly. Then, it would have to be rebroken in order to reset the healing process—a process which could take a human nearly a year, or weeks in my father's case. An inheritance of my mother's blood, as I have just described, was not something my father's metabolism would experience. He hated me for it—as it was something in my blood he could not control—but also for having an advantage that he did not.

I did not react further but kept my eyes locked with his. He decided to punish me, and that meant removing my sole comfort in the room. "Leave us, witch!" he hissed at Jacques.

My heart squeezed, tightening further with the anxiety I felt in my chest. As previously mentioned, it was not that Jacques could prevent what was coming by way of verbal and physical abuse, but his presence nonetheless gave me comfort. My father, along with all his villainy, was cunning and educated. He knew how to hurt me most, and right now he intended for that harm to be uninterrupted. This meant removing Jacques. I do not think my father was capable of understanding the depth of our relationship, but he did know I was weaker when Jacques was removed from my side.

To his credit, Jacques did not immediately move from his post beside me. Ever calm, he never had been intimidated—that I could tell at least—by my father. In a quite casual manner, he bent down and picked up the weight, looking it over for a moment before speaking.

"I think I will tend to this matter, Master, and see that it is cleaned properly and returned. Excuse me for a moment."

He turned on his heel and left the office, presumably to do just that. Although I was left alone now before my father and his clerk, to me, Jacques' words meant that he would not be far. Once the path before me was endured, he would be there beside me once again.

With a flick of his wrist and a small spark of his red-colored magic, Ward closed the door behind Jacques. This earned another grin from my father and emphasized the point that I had no escape. Clearing his throat, Ward dipped his pen into the fountain before positioning it above his note. He looked through his spectacles, perched on the bridge of his crooked nose, offering an inclination that my father could begin. It was a cursed dance they shared, and they knew one another's steps perfectly, anticipating each other's movement as they amused themselves with my suffering.

"Tell me what the bill is for, that you brought to my attention earlier, Ward..." My father snarled, dragging the tip of his claw against his desk, the noise alone causing me to clench my jaw. The slow sound of the wood splintering on his desk made my sensitive ears ache.

"Ah, yes," Ward began, pulling a paper up and off his podium. The pair played with their prey, and Ward did this by taking a moment to adjust his spectacles. Focusing on the words of the document he held, he cleared his throat once more, then spoke. "It was from the racing grounds, your lordship. It seems to be a reservation. Two, at that, were made for tomorrow—pardon, *today*—in the Avalone name. Two adjacent boxes with food and drink for four."

He paused with his vile, blunt tongue flicking out like that of a snake, to wet his lips before continuing. "The offices of the grounds found it quite strange, given that it was not your regular box, and wanted to confirm the request before invoicing for it." As he spoke, the witch wrote down his shorthand notes, setting the paper to the side. He smacked his lips and turned to my father, "I, too, found this strange, your lordship, as I had not seen such a request, per *your* request, recently pass my desk..."

"No, indeed!" My father growled in response. He rose to his feet, claws digging into his desktop, and he narrowly stared down at me. Similarly to the bears he resembled, he looked much larger when he stood and swelled in his anger. "So imagine my surprise when it was my bastard son's hand who signed the papers!"

He bellowed, hand swiping across his desk. Documents, ink and other supplies tumbled to the ground. Next, he grabbed the desk itself, and with his strength tossed it to the side as if it weighed nothing. Bear-like claws lengthened on his right hand, which swiped out at me as his thunderous and hateful voice shouted again.

"Without so much as a simple request for the permission to *DO SO!* You go behind my back and spend *MY* money!" With another swipe of his arm, now transformed into that of a large ursus, he caught my face and tore large gashes into the flesh of my cheek.

I couldn't help the sound of pain that escaped my lips. I was blinded momentarily from the blood that splattered my vision. Of course, I healed quickly after the blow, but that did not remove the pain till it was healed completely. I remained frozen, out of debilitating anxiety and trembling breath. Even if I could run, I wouldn't get far with him in this state. A few slaps and scratches were better than him literally mauling me halfway down the hall—something which he had done to others who displeased him before.

Ward quietly scratched out notes, an ominous scribbling sound that played in the background of my pain. A content little sneer tugged at the corners of his lips. He enjoyed my beating nearly every bit as much as my father did, though he did not mask it or twist it behind a barbaric lesson. It was plainly witnessed, and he observed with the same rapture of a schoolboy.

"Then I call for you, to question and scold...but you arrive, and you smell *DISGUSTING!*"

With the last insult, he punched me in the gut, knocking the wind from my lungs and causing me to stumble back. My knees became weak, and I fell onto them, gasping for air. Of course, his words were ruthless and nothing more than gaslight lies. He never would call me in here to simply question and scold. The plan all along was to bruise and beat me.

"Please, father— " I was silenced by his knee snapping up into my face, my nose breaking, and I spewed blood down the front of my shirt.

"Like a fucking buck in rut, every inch of you smells like it! Couldn't you even have the decency or evolved thought to clean yourself before coming into my presence?" He asked, though rhetorically.

Why hadn't I just kept my mouth shut? It's so much worse when I try to talk. I could no longer cry at this treatment, having faced this abuse and been degraded in this manner for years. Even so, my eyes did burn, a lump rising in my throat and threatening to come out as a whimper. I switched tactics, tried to appear submissive, to play into and please his alpha side. I had to show that I had no will nor desire to fight against him. It hurt my very bones to do so, but next he would start breaking limbs if I did not, so it was better to cause myself discomfort.

Large white wolf ears replaced my own, and they pinned back against my skull. I lowered myself to the ground and looked up through my lashes, letting out a small keening whine for good measure. My tail, too, was tucked between my legs. My body was trembling, though not intentionally, which helped get the point across. He growled lowly in my face, spittle flying onto my cheek, and there he remained as he hissed into my ear. His physical assault paused as he spoke, his voice low and guttural as his muzzle transformed into that of a bear.

"Just whom are you spending my money to attend the races with?" he snarled, his paw threading into my white hair and digging into my scalp. "*WHO?*" he shouted in my ear, paining me as I winced with another whine.

"L-Lady Evelyn, f-father," I responded with a trembling and weak voice. "W-Womanly company for her a-and a g-gentleman for myself—" My blubbering was cut off as my father wrenched me to my feet, using only my hair and ears to achieve this.

"*YOU* don't have friends. Who is this 'gentleman' you have invited on my pocketbook?"

Now, both standing, he wrenched my head back, and I gasped from the blinding pain.

"Of the C-Cartwright family, C-C-Charon," I squawked out in my desperation for the pain to end, body quaking. I was on the edge of either bawling, pissing myself or both—my bed clothes soaked already in my blood.

"*A FRENCHMAN—*" He began to shout, nearly about to bite my head off and perhaps end my life right there, when the door was knocked on and thrown open. In the doorway stood Jacques, the paperweight in his hands polished and bright.

"Pardon my intrusion, lord, but I have completed my task..."

The room paused as he walked forward. He looked around to see the state of it, which had been meticulous before but was now a chaotic disaster. Items and the desk had been strewn across the floor and covered in my blood. With a wave of his hand and without word, everything jumped back to its place of belonging. Like time had been rewound, the desk rolled back into place. Its flung contents fluttered back, too, and settled on the surface. Even the gouged scratch marks filled with the splinters as they returned from where they were littered over the floor. Jacques then stepped forward, placing the small weight back on the desk, adjusting it once, twice, then nodding in satisfaction of his work.

Next, he turned, looking between my father and my bloodied self. His head and shoulders perked up as a thought crossed his mind. He spoke, "I don't believe the Charrons are fully French, my lord. Maybe in part the heir...but I do believe they bought the company from the wife's family and simply kept the name for its notoriety."

He turned to Ward, who evidently had become bored with my beating and Jacques' reappearance. Having moved on to multitask with some other paperwork, Ward licked and smacked his lips again before nodding.

Ward looked at my father, "I believe that is correct, your lord-ship. They do all business from here in London. You have been meaning to commission them, too, I believe..."

The game had come to an end. I was beaten to submission and left lesser for it. My father had won, though the checkmate this time belonged to Jacques. He smiled proudly, feigning the pleasure of having been of assistance to my father. Jacques snapped his fingers then, and I was suddenly behind him.

"Surely, we have taken up too much of your valuable time this morning, so I will retire the boy to his quarters..." His magic froze my tongue, then made me bow to Ward, then my father. He also freely did this action with me before speaking up one last time. "Do you wish me to handle the notification of cancelling the outing then?" He seemingly asked both father and Ward, again speaking as if in-debted to this favor for them, and this played to their egos well.

My father deflated, his body returning to its natural state as he rounded his desk to sit down. He'd had his fill of beating me, and without further egging on from his clerk, he too had lost interest in continuing. He began to speak, but Ward had beaten him to it with his own suggestion and opinion. "Wouldn't it be better to incur the debt of the Charrons, my lord? Allow this childish outing, but keep the favor to be returned by the family at a later date?"

My father grumbled in thought, stroking his crooked chin be-fore eventually waving a hand in approval. "See that it's document-ed, Ward," he responded as Jacques' and my presence was forgotten.

Hearing this, Jacques spared not a second longer to linger—his magic pushing me out into the hallway as he followed. He bowed upon leaving, then joined me in the hall as Ward's red magic closed the door behind us.

CHAPTER 8

Now in the hall, my knees felt weak again, and I reached out to Jacques for stability or to catch me should I fall. His strong capable arm was offered, to which I clung as he raised a finger to his lips. We would need to silently leave this wing of the estate or face the newly charged aggravation of my father. Then he swung my arm over him, and he supported me as we withdrew to my quarters.

I slumped my weight against Jacques, finally taking a deep, ragged breath. My lungs burned as they filled with air, apparently having held my breath through most of the encounter with my father. My lip trembled, tears now filling my eyes at the overwhelming relief I felt in the realization that the confrontation was over. In the last year, I had seen my father less than a handful of times, but each chronicled visit had been worse than the one previous. Till tonight, where I had been practically beaten to unconsciousness.

"Shh, let us get you to your room, young lord," Jacques' calm voice gently soothed me. He easily held my weight as we moved, finally crossing over into 'my' corner of the estate. "It is over now, let us clean you up and return to bed."

I could only nod in response, clinging to him and following his lead. The relief I felt was momentary, as it transformed into a numb state of being. I felt as if my consciousness had begun separating from myself, like my soul was splitting from my beaten and bruised physical body to a separate, uninjured form. The feeling was terrifying, yet desirable. I hated myself, I hated this life of torture. I watched a few steps behind Jacques and myself as he brought me to my room and sat me down. My large, sluggish unblinking eyes looked up at the witch.

Jacques' touch was compassionate, delicately turning my compliant face back and forth. His clement blue eyes observed my broken nose. Seeing the vacant state of my eyes, he let out a short sigh and tried to offer a reassuring smile, but it was full of sadness.

"Come back to me, Thaddeus...We have to reset your nose, and I need you present for that." He softly spoke, holding my face, cradling it, and brushing his thumb over the newly healed skin of my cheek. The action brought me back to the present, and Jacques' smile warmed, seeing the light enter my eyes again.

"Can you set it back?" I asked, head tilting in his hands.

"Welcome back," Jacques cooed in encouragement. He turned my head back and forth once again before curtly nodding. "Yes, I think we can get it back into place...though, it will hurt..." Noting my hesitancy, he added, "I can do it quickly."

A trembling breath escaped me as I nodded, my shoulders slumping forward. Though painful to correct, an ugly and crooked nose was going to earn me no favors. At worst, it would invite innocent questions from those who did not understand. So I looked up at Jacques, feeling my eyes burn again. Tears threatened to tumble down onto my cheeks, which were caked with dried blood.

"Nothing more than a quick discomfort, and it will be set again..." His thumb gently ran along the crooked bridge of my nose, and I could feel as he cast a spell, helping to numb the olfactory area of my face. He distracted me with his mild words, "I've already had a bath drawn, and once we—"

Jacques suddenly grabbed hold of my nose and, with a loud crack, snapped it back into place. I winced, trying to flinch away as my eyes squeezed shut. Tears escaped, but he firmly held me in place, keeping my nose braced as the fragile bones rapidly began to heal again.

"There, there, it's done. That's all for the pain..." he assured. "Let's give a moment for this to heal. The bath is drawn, so you can get cleaned up in private and I will use the time to prepare your bed..."

From rebreaking my nose, a small clot of blood dislodged and trickled down my lip. Jaques brought up a kerchief and wiped it away—a somewhat futile task, given the bloodied and destroyed state of my bed clothes. Still, even through tear-filled eyes, I could see that he was trying to provide every comfort he could. It hurt me more than any wound my father cast onto my skin, that I was such a pathetic burden for Jacques to take care of.

My lip trembled as the words poured forth before I thought them through, "I'm so sorry for the inconvenience I have caused you..."

Jacques' brow furrowed, and he let out a displeased *harrumph* in response to my apology. "You hold your tongue. I have no need to be apologized to, Thaddeus. While this may be a job, as I have said before, it is one I do with honor." His face softened, slowly letting my nose go to cradle my face again. He gave my face the smallest shake as he scolded me lightheartedly, "None of this is your fault, and you deserve none of the abuse bestowed on you. Never apologize for their actions unto you."

I could not keep his intimately held gaze, and my amber eyes tore away from his aged blue. My lip quivered again, lips parting, but there was nothing I could say. For, agreeing would be dishonest, as I did harbor the feelings of these incidents being entirely my fault.

Jacques saw this and sighed quietly. He pulled me into him, in such a manner that I could pull away should I wish to, but at this moment it was not something I could deny. His embrace was affectionate and inviting—a place I could hide. I buried my face into his shoulder, sobs ripping from my throat as I quaked from my crying fit. Jacques said no more words, silently holding me and allowing me to shed my tears. His hand tenderly slid up the back of my head, smoothing down the ruffled and torn hair.

I couldn't control it, with everything being so overwhelming at that moment. My tears wetted his shoulder, and my bloody snot stained the fabric of his robe. Without judgement, he quietly allowed me to release my pain and emotions, letting it all out in the safe embrace of his arms. The pressure built, escaping before it could begin rotting out my insides.

This episode lasted a dozen or so minutes, my forlorn wails simmering into small whimpers and attempts to catch my breath. With tenderness, he lightly danced his fingers through my hair, helping to calm me. Even after I made no further audible sounds of despair, Jacques allowed me to hide in his hold till I felt ready to emerge again. This I indulged in, until the scent of my own blood and tears was replaced by his smokey cinnamon scent.

A wave of fatigue washed over me then, parting from him as my eyes remained downcast to the floor. His aged hand brushed my hair back once more, till his hand settled on the nape of my neck. He held me there, forehead brushing against mine. "Bath?"

he asked in a hushed tone. Not intending to push me, he benignly
reminded me of the option.

I nodded, silent. I had no more words, and my every effort con-
centrated on not collapsing to the bed. He stood, bringing me with
him and supporting me. I was navigated to the ensuite of my room,
where once the door was opened, steam billowed out like a rolling fog. He used steady gestures, tapping my breast and signaling
that I should give him my bloodied clothes. I stripped, pulling the
robe off first, then my sleeping attire. I handed it off to Jacques and
turned to the tub.

It was the largest slipper-style tub available to me. Made of cop-
per, the metal could hold the boiled water's heat—and so for my
protection, a yard of fabric had been cast over the tub. It had settled
down into the water now, and the bath's steaming, bubbled surface
called to my aching body. Jacques did pause, seeing if I needed assistance with entering the tub. As I moved forward, he knew aid was
not required and left. He quietly closed the door behind himself
and left me with my privacy.

Holding the side, I swung one leg over, then the second, and
submerged myself in the water. The temperature was perfect—
nearly scalding—and quickly pinkened my skin. The blood that
had dried on my forearms disappeared as the water touched it,
bubbles surrounding me and doubling in number from the movement of my entering. I closed my eyes, resting my head back before
sinking below the surface.

The searing water gradually washed away the physical signs of
my father's abuse. Bruises had already faded, wounds healed and
thus evidence sealed. Even my nose, which only moments prior
had been rebroken to set, showed no outward appearance of damage. Only a dull ache persisted that made my tired eyes weep from

the pressure. I lay there, weightless, letting my exterior be cleansed. Exhaustion made my eyelids heavy, and the only sound under the water was my own heartbeat.

Alone, warm and safe for the moment, a picture of the human came to my mind. Atlas, with his bright, smiling face and flirtatious ways. I still would get to see him at the races, I realized. I was drawn to him. For as sordid and abysmal as my life was, someone whose very soul glowed as bright as his was captivating. As the waters washed away my wounds, his presence in my head made me forget everything else but him. I smiled at the picture of him in my mind's eye and kept that close to my heart. My father could beat me, even kill me if he wished, but what my mind held he could not touch. My soul he could not destroy. Even after this latest occurrence, I could further defy him and experience happiness.

I rose above the water, satisfied with my cleansed state. Before the water could cool and give me a chill, I crawled out of the tub, briskly drying off. At the sound of my exiting the tub, Jacques knocked and entered with new sleeping clothes in hand that he helped dress me in. The fabric was toasty and crisp, likely heated by the hearth till I was ready.

He still did not speak, though in my exhausted state, I do not know if I even would have had energy to reply. So for the better, he returned to the bedroom, leaving the door open to the ensuite. He had made my bed—new sheets ready to tuck myself into, the handle of two warming pans peeking out from the side. He grabbed these and removed them as I approached. Slipping under the sheets, I was enveloped by the bed's comfort.

Immediately as my head hit the pillow, my eyes shut. I let out a shaky breath and settled in, pulling the blankets up and under my chin, already on my way to sleep. Jacques leaned down, brushing back my damp hair. The faint, static feeling of his magic danced over my skull—my hair instantly drying—and Jacques hummed in satisfaction.

"Sleep, young lord. Regain your strength, and I will wake you in time for your outing tomorrow."

He may have also cast a sleeping spell upon me. Although I can't be sure, my sleep was peaceful that remaining night, and my dreams were loving. They were of Atlas' sweet lips on my skin kissing away every ache, my own lips buried in his blonde hair.

CHAPTER 9

The racing grounds were abuzz with activity and merriment, a hub of gambling and other various socialite enterprises. This sport attracted the most elite of society, while at the same time attracting those of lesser standing as well. As with any event that will accommodate ale and wager, the crowds did come. Such activity made the witching hour affair fade away, like it had instead been a horrible nightmare that was endured and slowly forgotten. No bruises, nor even a crooked nose, were left to remember it by. So although it was unhealthy to do so, I treated it as such and let it be forgotten.

The crowd was particularly ample today, and the balmy fall weather promised quite a pleasant day of sun, yet with enough breeze to allow for comfort with a jacket. My carriage rattled up to the drop-off—Jacques in my attendance as we descended from the behemoth transport. The activities and bodily movement seemed to fade away from my attention, my heart fluttering at the prospect of Atlas' company and filling my chest with nervous excitement. Such yearnings were confirmed at the sight of his family's coach parked yonder. However, I did remain composed, retaining an air of nobility merely for the benefit of onlookers, despite my fluttering rise of elation within.

My focus was singularly upon the arrival of my guests. Everything else seemed to pass unnoticed, though I understood how the events should theoretically have been unfolding. Tickets ought to have been retrieved leading up to the private viewing boxes, where a few passing introductions or short conversations would be exchanged.

Arriving early to these events allowed for the socially elite to dine or converse business, eyeing up the equine and placing one's bets. My focus, though, was upon my guests and greeting them. Admittedly, one particular guest ultimately took precedence. A small corridor led up to our rented perch, a small trek I had to will myself to take nonchalantly.

Each step seemed harder than the last to remain steadily ascendant, and it felt like an eternity before I finally stepped back up into the light of the late-August sun. Atlas would not be alone, as in the booth adjacent would be Lady Marquardt and whomever she invited as well. Perhaps yes, I was indulging my desire for closeness to the charming lord, but this was also to be a public display of my support to Evelyn and my own engagement. Above all else, I needed—demanded of myself—to keep my wits.

My feet finally landed upon the final steps leading up to my reserved box. I gave a curt shake of my head, trying to clear away my eagerness as I ascended the stands. Reaching the top step, the intensity of the midday sun blinded me for a moment. The murmurs of those conversing in other booths filled my hearing, along with a light breeze fluttering through the stands.

"Ah, Thaddeus!" the human's voice rang out, and my eyes were quick to adjust to the lighting. Atlas leaned against the rung that separated the booths, having been holding a conversation with Lady Marquardt and her guest before my appearance.

Upon my arrival the three individuals stood, Atlas stepping to the side so as for me to greet my fiancée. Lady Marquardt and her guest dipped down into curtsies, which I returned with a bow. I gently took Evelyn's hand, placing a benign kiss upon it. With each and every movement or action committed, I could feel Atlas' eyes upon me, watching me. I did everything to tame the joy that was bubbling up inside, for I needed to remain neutral in outward emotions in such a public place.

"What a pleasure it is to be invited out like this, Thaddeus," Evelyn said as she brought her hand back, folding them before her abdomen. She held her head proudly, gazing at me with her muted brown eyes. A great appreciation was shown in them, ringing her words thankful and true. "We have been blessed by the day's weather."

I nodded to her, a smile coming to my face. Evelyn was easier to talk to than most individuals. "Yes, we really are," I replied to her, my eyes drifting to the lady she brought for company, prompting an introduction.

"In my company today is Miss Agatha Dravenstebt, a very close friend of mine since our childhood," Evelyn spoke boldly as she introduced her friend. "Our families have been very close for many generations."

"A pleasure, Lord Avalone," Lady Marquardt's company dropped into another low curtsey. Both the ladies were dressed in simpler attire, my fiancée cloaked in subtle grey tones—simple and refined, as often her family would dress. Miss Agatha, however, wore more color, including green hues throughout her ensemble that made her similarly colored eyes sparkle from her freckled face. Her red hair—which was obviously a terror to tame—was braided back against her skull, and her surname finally clicked.

In noble supernatural families, the employment of a witch, mage or less common wizard was an all-important position to fill. This was especially true for the youth and younger members of a family, as the witches' powers and cloaking spells were a great asset to concealing their true forms. For my family, Jacques held that title, and his duty was to accompany me—as I was the youngest member in his charge—in case of such an incident where his talents were required. The Dravenstebts were a talented family of witches, revered as *geniuses* in their fields of study, particularly alchemy.

History would state that witches were tortured, burned and massacred. Without debate, these atrocities did occur, but witches are smart and despotic. It must be understood, therefore, that no actual magic-possessing witch was damned by mere human hand. Nor could any real supernatural creature be so absolutely exposed without consent of the region's alpha, such as my father. If humans were to condemn, torture and execute a true witch, it was ordered by the alpha and planned. It was a layer of protection for supernatural beings, the false persecution of humans in place of actual creatures. To those in power, humans were mere chattel, simply used and disposed of. The Dravenstebts were of lower nobility, but nonetheless were a great and powerful asset.

"It is wonderful to make your acquaintance, Miss Dravenstebt," I warmly greeted, turning to the side now to greet Atlas.

This was the first time my eyes finally landed on his form this day, and he was exquisite to behold. He wore black attire, with every trim and lapel vibrantly golden. He seemed to almost gleam, my breath stolen by his lavish beauty. My heart hammered in my chest like a relentless blacksmith pounding on an anvil. His hair was held back from his face this time, exposing his beautiful depthless blue eyes that pierced deep into my own masked brown. Everything seemed to happen automatically, muscle memory taking over my actions from the years of etiquette grooming.

"I see you have met my friend, Atlas Charron," I stated. Atlas' eyes pierced deep into my flesh, his hand reaching out and grasping mine, and he shook it in greeting.

"Wonderful as always, Thaddeus. I am so *very* glad you took me up on my offer for us to attend the races together," he said as his lip curled into a satisfied smirk.

Just as our physical contact was about to break, he gave my hand another lingering squeeze, softly stroking his thumb against my skin. It was a small, hidden action that invigorated my soul. My weak heart could not take any more, and with inner reluctance I released his hand. I was flustered, despite my best efforts to keep a calm head. Atlas' pleased smirk only grew as he easily brought the attention of our party to himself, providing a moment or two for me to compose myself.

"It has been an absolute pleasure speaking with Lady Marquardt and Miss Dravenstebt. They are both very smart and beautiful ladies to converse with." Atlas chuckled, and the ladies giggled as well. His charismatic attitude and accompanying smile lit up the space effortlessly, a quality that made me yearn to have him closer.

We took our seats, and beverages were provided. Small morsels were also set at our tables, and our own conversations ensued. Most attendees enjoyed a small meal and relaxed conversation before the stands came deafeningly to life. Then, it was time to place one's bets.

Publicly, this appeared to be an outing orchestrated by myself, supporting the relationship between Evelyn and myself but respectfully remaining out of one another's touch till our marriage bed. Deep down I knew it was a ruse, and while I did feel guilt, the thrill of having the man I was infatuated with sitting across the table from me chased away those emotions. Especially in that moment, with the teasing tip of his shoe on my calf, he blew away all emotion other than my endearment for him. Atlas simply sipped his drink, eyes fixed upon me, challenging me to speak first. I partook in a small sandwich, trying to remove the lump that had arisen in my throat, rendering me mute.

Finally, I found my voice and addressed the human. "It has been too long," I managed to get out, my voice cracking. Dammit.

"Was it because of regret?" Atlas leisurely questioned, gazing over the rim of his cup, sparkling blue eyes lit with life. His question made my throat want to close off, to suffocate and waste away to nothing. That was not the case, though. It was nerves, it was my own insecurities, it was his miniscule knowledge of the world around him.

"Not at all," I gasped, voice steady. My eyes burned as I looked to him, until they fell to the side, a gesture to my fiancée seated behind me. "I have been confused, if I am being honest with you. The decision between duty and desire...It weighs heavily upon me."

Atlas paused at my words, color flushing his cheeks slightly as he cleared his throat. It was his turn to be speechless, but he was quick to the recover. Atlas' eyes looked deeply into my own.

"You find me desirable?" he asked with a teasingly tenor voice.

"Undeniably," I responded, taking a sip from my cup of tea. It did help a bit in soothing my palate, as the mouthful of dry cotton I seemingly swallowed that made speaking an insurmountable task waned in its potency. "Such is the case, but it does not make me oblivious to the dangerous matter that this creates for both of us. Not to mention, it could very quickly affect and poison those close to us."

As forementioned, same-sex couples were and *are* a possibility in the community of supernatural creatures—with but two caveats. First is the use or possibility of reproduction for reason in the coupling. Far more dangerous, though, was the mundane opinion. To the mundane, this was a crime against nature and their God. Punishable by torture and sometimes even death, it was an unforgiveable taboo. Supernatural creatures, however, already held such secrecy about their existence, so what was one more sub-rosa detail? Atlas was aware of the hellfire this could bring, and yet still under cover of the table dressings, he teased my leg in the most intimate way.

Atlas' hesitation was absent as he took note of my inner turmoil and spoke, "Well then, we better come up with one hell of an alibi for our close and constant communication, shall we not?" His suggestion was accompanied by a feline-like grin, snatching up a tea sandwich and biting into it.

He was daring and fearless, such a stance one could only take—supernatural or mundane—if they were unreservedly passionate. His words, cockily stated, held much in the weight of fact to our situation. What reason would the son of a carriage-maker—though wealthy and revered for their artistry, nonetheless—have for interacting with a youth of nobility, other than just the former's craft? Surely, it would give reason for communication during construction of the transport, but projects do come to an end, and the reason would become void.

"Indeed, it will need to be." I smirked over the brim of my cup.

The stands filled around us as our conversation of plot ensued. For the long game, we did not have answers, nor any thought process as to what we would do come that time when we no longer had a suitable excuse for our correspondence. Youthful naivety was the culprit. For the present, however, it was all too easy to construct a reason for further acquaintance. I would commission the Charron family for the production of a carriage for my bride-to-be. After all, a perfect wedding gift would constitute many meetings and long appointments with one another.

The risk involved would be prodigious, but the thrill of unbridled proximity trounced any logical sense. Atlas' eyes were shimmering with life, smiles of delight curling on both our lips. It was effortless communicating with each other—a buzz of warmth filling my chest as laughter came easily.

With cups emptied and food consumed, the race would soon begin. Our conversation paused as Atlas looked around, a suspicious grin splitting across his face as he looked over my form to Evelyn and her own talking partner. Before I could question him and his dubious grin, he arose from his chair, snatching the pamphlet listing the day's racers. He stepped toward Evelyn and Agatha.

"Ladies," he permissively purred, his beam continuing to grow across his face while he fanned himself with the leaflet. "With the apex of today's events impending, Thaddeus and myself find ourselves apt to place wagers on the upcoming thoroughbred, Featherdance. Could we take your wagers down to the offices as well?"

The women giggled behind their fans, brows raising and whispering secrets. I rose from my chair with an amused simper upon my face. Agatha spoke and manifested her purse from the folds of her skirt, pulling notes from within it. "We wager quite differently than yourself and Lord Thaddeus. In fact, the veteran thoroughbred, Corporal, retains our support." She held out her fare, smirking at the human who was already feeling triumphant over his decision.

He gave a light nod, "Let the beasts then decide who is right." He cheekily goaded, earning a mild scoff from the witch.

"Yes, let's. I will enjoy collecting your money as my own," Agatha further chided Atlas as we descended from the box.

~

The races soon would commence, and as a result, the betting offices overflowed with bodies and screaming voices. It did prove to be a nearly uncomplicated task for the human. Atlas was light and nimble on his feet, effortlessly maneuvering through the crowds and reaching the front line to place our bets. Tickets in hand, he returned to my side, and I presumed we would head back to our box. Figures were flooding past us, the gates moments away from releasing. We hastened our pace, trying to get back to our posting.

Suddenly, I was thrust backwards by a strong hand pulling me by the clothing. I was thrown back into what appeared to be a storage closet of sorts, filled with roping and canvas and other miscellaneous items. Such details were cast aside, however, as my assailant was none other than Atlas Charron, and he was locking the door behind him.

I suppose for a human, suddenly being shoved into a closet would be a more difficult situation in which to remain calm. The room was devoid of light, and were it not for my supernatural status, perhaps fear would be present. As it were, seeing in the dark was as natural for me as seeing in the daylight. It was, however, quite comical to see his human pupils blown wide—the organ's best effort to see in this space—his arms awkwardly reaching out for me. I could not help as a light chortle bubbled up from my chest, watching him move closer.

"Just what are you doing?" I asked, my voice alerting him to my exact location.

The human boldly surged forward, his body pressing against mine. His lips pressed hard against my neck as I felt his hot breath. I was utterly stunned into speechlessness—though without a doubt, I was euphorically pleased by this quick turn of events as I was fondled feverishly.

"I am ravaging you," he heatedly whispered into my ear, pressing a hot kiss to its shell. "I receive silence for weeks, and then you call upon me, wearing these tight clothes and fluttering your eyelashes. It's maddening!"

Our lips collided, and unlike the first kiss we shared, this was rushed, *lustful*. Hands on one another, I clung to the front of his clothing. We barely breathed as we devoured each other.

"Then you casually, over *tea*—in front of your *betrothed*—plot our courting as if it is so simple," his breaths were rapid.

His advances paused as he harshly caught his breath. Atlas nuzzled his face against mine, and I did the same in return. I did not have words that could answer his accusations. Nor would I be able to effectively communicate them if I did, as his closeness was exquisitely suffocating, and my tongue could not loosen except to dance along his. My fervent actions would need to display my feelings regarding our unique situation.

His taste was so sweet and delicious as his lips seared against mine, and it felt *good* to let the human devour and blind my senses. I understood Atlas, as well as the desire as I felt for him just as strongly. He absolutely fascinated me. The way he took effortless charge of conversations, his confident smile—these qualities perhaps I desired to have within myself. Many of the attributes he possessed, I wanted to claim as my own.

What I desired most, in this moment, was not to see him as strong. I wanted to have him yield to my advance. In the back of my mind, I knew this was the beast within me, the alpha creature wanting to take control. I was also hyperaware of my physical illusion nearing its limitations.

When the elevation of hormones was present in creatures of my kind (as such, it was not the only thing elevated at this moment) it could be much harder to retain one's mundane appearance. My teeth ached as fangs wanted to bite into my dear one's shoulder, temples throbbing as ears sought to transform and press back against my skull. My spine shuddered as a tail longed to sprout forth and wag. It was a burning ache, the magic of Garmr preventing all this while I was so aroused. A small growl escaped me as I changed our positions, hurriedly grasping his hands and pinning them above his head.

"*Slow down,*" I snarled, pressing my face to his neck as we both panted. "Neither time...Nor place..." I breathlessly warned, earning an impish little giggle from the human.

"Quite, quite," he affirmed my words, his chest heaving against my own.

I glanced up from his shoulder, still pinning his hands. His face was flushed aggressively, blonde hair a wild mess and...He was stunning. His eyes closed—delicate, full eyelashes daintily laid—as he awaited his fate. I pressed a kiss to his cheek, and then a nervous laugh bubbled up within me as I pressed my forehead to his. I released his hands, and his actions mirrored my own as they dropped to rest on my shoulders. Our eyes locked, and we soaked up the sight of one another.

Suddenly, we were made very aware of our surroundings—cheers deafened us, and the wooden stands shook from its power. We both looked up towards the noise and quickly looked back to each other. Atlas nearly busted a gut, clapping my shoulder with his hand, throwing his head back as he bounced lightly.

"We seem to have missed the race! Surely, we will be missed and must pause this till next time, my dear." The human drew me in for a tight hug.

My heart burned with despair from the reality of needing to separate from one another. I held Atlas close, breathing in his scent. "Soon," I quietly begged him, pressing my lips to his ear desperately.

The human squeezed me tightly to himself, releasing a muffled groan and nodding, "Yes soon, Thaddeus. Now go, and try your best not to be suspicious! I will follow," he assured me with a light chuckle, doing his best to smooth down my vest in this dim lighting.

How my heart ached and wanted nothing more than to stow away longer in this closet. Reality would not allow it, and the truth was that those who we escorted on this day would begin—if they had not already—searching for us. I could not part without one final kiss, however, so I dragged him in once more, claiming the human for myself as I stole his breath. I could feel his knees nearly buckle from this kiss, holding to my forearms for support. It could not last, as time was against us. Having more brains than I, Atlas did not let it last long. A small groan fell from his gorgeously plumped lips.

"You must go," he weakly spoke.

I nodded, for he was right that we could not linger. I held the side of his burning face, gingerly gliding my thumb along it, while my other hand was already placed on the door and ready to bolt.

"I will call upon you soon," I guaranteed him.

He nodded, giving my hand a final squeeze before letting it go and shooing me with a love-drunk smile plastered onto his face.

I cracked the door open and peered out into the light. The lower parts of the stadium were bustling with activity once more—

those who won their bets flooding to collect. I easily slipped out unnoticed and made my way back to the hall that would bring myself to our box. Along the way, I gathered from overheard conversations that the race had been no contest. Corporal, the veteran thoroughbred, had taken the win. It would be quite a delight to see Agatha harassing Atlas in a few moments over her triumph.

I rounded the corner, finding the correct stairwell. There, I paused took a moment to dust off and straighten myself up in an attempt to not look so ravaged. Once satisfied with my appearance, I turned to head up the stairwell but had to take yet another pause. Halfway up, there were two figures—one leaned over the other, embracing as they giggled in excitement. It was Agatha and Evelyn in a state of joy from their victory and winnings. They had not noticed me, evidently, as Agatha pulled back from their embrace to heatedly kiss Evelyn.

My jaw dropped as they pulled apart, gazing happily into each other's eyes. It was an all too familiar gaze, one that I myself had been conducting mere moments before. In my shock, I did not make a sound, nor did I notice—despite my keen senses—as Atlas came up behind me, witnessing this intimacy between the two women. Atlas sneered, his hands resting on his hips.

The pair and I did notice, however, when the human suddenly blurted out, "I *knew* it!" Atlas heartily howled at his discovery. Words were unforthcoming as I looked between him and the women.

The pair instantly pushed apart from one another, and Atlas was tickled pink into momentary silence. Evelyn could not make eye contact with anyone, and her sight remained downcast, seemingly wanting to melt into the shadows. Agatha's own eyes hardened, narrowing as she glowered at the human. Both the women, without a doubt, thought they had destroyed or at the very least heavily damaged the engagement.

Perhaps they thought I would run to my father, enraged by Evelyn's impurity. Perhaps they thought I would run to *her* father, demanding to have it called off. This poisonous apple would rot the tree, her entire family disgraced, and I am sure my silent, shocked reaction did nothing but fuel these fires.

Then there was the matter of the human—*my* human—who had borne witness and might speak of the scandal. Because of him, a whole additional layer of terror would be present in their minds. Unaware of my own scandalous relationship with him, they were left to try and conceal two supposedly condemnable traits.

All of this being the case, it was Agatha who rushed down the stairs toward Atlas with rage and fear behind her eyes. She raised her hand, ready to cast a spell, with every intent to destroy this human who saw them embracing. My feet moved before my brain could think, stepping in front of the witch.

My teeth bared in warning as I guarded him, "He is *MINE!*"

Her hand stayed, both females' eyes widening at my words. Garmr burned upon my hand, but the pain was nothing as the adrenaline coursed through my veins. Witches were not typically creatures that bent to the order of an alpha, but Evelyn's kind was. Her head lowered immediately at my display of intimidation and aggression.

"Are you *suicidal*?" Agatha hissed into my face, rage overcoming her fear. "He can't—"

Atlas suddenly was at our sides, his arm coming between our rigid forms, an elfin smile on his face. Thanks to magic charms and trinkets, we only appeared as two livid humans, despite what was truly occurring—a beast and witch going for each other's throats.

Atlas casually spoke, "Come now, we are making a scene. Let us cool our heads and reconvene on another day to discuss this matter." Agatha cast a look of disgust down on him, recoiling and taking a step back up the stairs as he stood between her and myself. The charming human took no offense, quickly adding on for the volatile witch's ease of conscience, "For it seems we all have a commonality that could surely doom us for social guillotine."

If it were not for the high stakes of the moment, I would have found his brazen dictation of the conversation amusing. Agatha did falter when he spoke, realizing what he was getting at. His hands gestured from ourselves to them with candor. Both the women's eyes blew wide open. Looking between us, their faces warmed to shades of red. Atlas held his head high with victory, offering his hand to Agatha to take our leave.

He suggested, "So let us collect your winnings, my dear. We shall take our leave, and we can all think on what has transpired. Don't you think it would be best to discuss it later.?"

Quite astounded, Agatha nodded, taking the human's arm as he led to make her collections. Evelyn's head remained downcast, descending the remaining stairs and coming to my side. I could smell a wave of anxiety and fear wafting off of her. I knew not what words could soothe her emotions, but I could only imagine the hopelessness and fear that bubbled up inside of her. If it was in any way a parallel to what I had felt myself, particularly since celebrating our third-party chosen engagement, she quite possibly felt as if she were suffocating.

As her gentle hand took hold of my arm, I placed my hand over hers, giving it a squeeze of comfort that I hoped might gain her eye contact. Her brown eyes did drift up to mine, but unlike myself, she hid every raw, burning emotion. This was a respectable trait and assured what I already knew. She was a strong and resilient woman.

"Evelyn, dear, I think what has happened is for the best." Facially, her calm facade did not waver, but she squeezed my arm a little tighter. I did pause here, giving a small sigh, for I wanted my words to be blunt and solidify my position in a way that offered solace to her. "You and I are both the same. We love and cherish one who is not the person to whom we are promised. I have no intent of forcing your consort away, and it is my wish that you do the same for my own." I made notice of her shuddering intake of breath from relief and added, "May she bring you happiness, but we will move forward with our marriage for publicity's sake—both your own and mine—and we shall prevail through this."

She nodded, expelling another sigh of relief.

"Yes, we shall."

CHAPTER 10

After the race, interaction was—for lack of better wording—awkward. So much had happened in a relatively short amount of time, and reflecting on it now, it seemed to occur in a blur. Our goodbyes were offered, everyone withdrawing for their carriages and leaving the grounds. Nerves remained, but I was optimistic about what was awaiting in our futures.

It had been four days since the races, and the quartet of us, at least to my ears, had been silent—no communication whatsoever. In the evening hours, my rising jitters were finally calmed when a letter was delivered.

Given that I was home for the day, my appearance was not controlled. Within the protection and guard of our abodes, many supernatural beings took their natural forms. Especially as a creature with a less-than anthropoid mien, I always chose not to constrict my appearance when possible. Maintaining a mundane appearance left a dull ache in my body, so on days such as these I sought not to. My white hair was tied back in a small bun, and I wore a simple linen shirt, trousers and bare feet. My long tail swayed behind me, the tip flicking back and forth, much like a cat's.

Jacques entered my study with a faint knock, drawing my attention away from the texts and lore I had poured over with hopes of distraction. "A letter has arrived for you, young lord. I have left it in the drawing room, along with some tea to wind down your evening."

Perhaps my reaction proved too eager, for I saw a glimmer of amusement in Jacques' expression. Given that I was never one to receive letters, this could only mean that this letter was a correspondence, finally, between the three individuals I attended the races with. Tail bobbing with as little enthusiasm as I could muster, I headed for the drawing room.

Jacques silently chuckled, as I was not convincing in appearing uninterested. He opened the door and gave a small teasing bow of his head as I entered the room, briskly stepping over to the table where the letter sat. The hearth contained a roaring fire, which cast dancing shapes onto the room's surfaces. Upon the table was a silver tray—tea setting for one of a teapot, one sole cup and plated pastries. I took a seat upon one of a pair of bergères, for upon the platter as well was a letter. The family initials pressed in wax were that of Atlas Charron.

My heart skipped a beat as I picked up the envelope and began breaking the seal to read its contents. The fragrance of scented oil flooded my senses, and I smiled at Atlas' familiar smell. Finally, I read.

Dearest Thaddeus,

I hope this letter finds you well, and that you have enjoyed yourself in the days since we last enjoyed each other's company at the races. I write to you in hope that you will receive my invitation to a salon at my family's primary townhome in Kensington on the fifth of

September. There is much to plan for your engagement soirée, and I have taken the liberty of inviting the Ladies Marquardt and Dravenstebt to attend as well.

The four of us might enjoy a brunch and begin preliminary discussions on important engagement party particulars.

Devotedly yours,
Atlas P. Charron.

I ran a hand back through my fair hair, rereading the document and sighing, as really there was no further hidden content I could decipher. In its simplicity, this was just a letter inviting me to a salon. One could interpret from the wording that he wished to become grand marshal for my engagement festivities, and this was his way of achieving this possibility. It was so short and to the point, however, that mentally I chastised myself for creating additional meaning. I doubted that any letter I may have written in those last few days would have been acceptable. I would have lengthily discussed much in the way of our personal matters, which if befallen into the wrong hands could have been disastrous for our party.

I settled back into my seat, taking up a cup of tea and sipping it as I watched the flames in the hearth dance and play, the wood popping as it burned—a soothing noise to me. I held the letter to my breast, and Atlas' scent flooding my sinuses. Finally having an answer about what may lie ahead, or rather a path to follow, did help to put my mind at ease.

Truthfully, I did not know what everyone's feelings were after we departed. I wondered if the days perhaps provided clarity for my three acquaintances, or if perhaps they—like myself—only discovered more questions and curiosities. Despite my hesitations, I also felt a weight lifted by what happened at the races. The burden of my duty and responsibility to Evelyn was now less so. The obvious factor was that neither of us had love for one another.

But in fact, both Evelyn and I *did* have someone we loved, and that jeopardized everything. My personal feeling was that our lives would become hell on earth if both or either of us created a scandal by refusing this arranged marriage. This being the case, I would not be the reason such horror would befall her. Nor, it seemed, would she do so to me.

Nevertheless, we had arrived at a difficult circumstance, for neither of us had been truthful to the other. I had made up my mind in these last few days that if we did pull through this together, I would always speak the truth to Evelyn in these matters of personal feelings. The engagement and our soon-to-be marriage were merely for our parents' benefit—nothing more than a business deal. It was our lives, so I wanted to do my part to minimize our suffering.

I leaned forward and placed the letter into the fire, watching as the parchment ignited and turned to ash. It was not something I should keep, for it could be used as evidence against me or the others. His perfect wording and scent were gone within a moment, reduced to nothing, and I was left to ponder what the day forward would bring.

~

The fifth of September was a beautiful autumn day. The sun shone brightly, bringing warmth to the earth, but a steady breeze prevented the day from becoming sweltering. I had informed Jacques of the salon when breakfast was brought to my room and tasked him with the necessary planning for my transportation.

He had a grin upon his face, as well as a particular happiness to his demeanor. He seemed proud that I was interacting with others my age—regardless of creature or mundane status, evidently. I was pleased with myself as well, for I knew it was not good to stay cooped up as I did. Though the topic of this salon would be nefarious discussions at best, for such an introverted creature as myself, it was a start.

Our manor was not too far from the Charrons' townhome, and thus only an hour before Atlas requested my presence, I set out in a carriage, accompanied by both Jacques and a driver. My aged retainer sat across from me, still wearing a comforted smile on his face. I simply shook my head at his enthusiasm, as truly it was in some ways a deceit to him and thus did not bode well with me. That said, I did let him have this moment, and within the back of my mind, I hoped that it would not turn into a bitter disappointment for him.

The carriage clattered up to his home, and unlike our gathering at the races, I seemed to have arrived before the ladies of our troupe. Jacques exited the transport and walked up to the grand entrance. Like most of the homes and buildings in this district, it was made of brick. Supplementing its lavish appearance was elegantly crafted white trim. The latter, I dare state, was grander than most for a townhome, and that could only serve as due credit to their business. A sign reading *"Charron and Sons Carriages"* acted as a sconce to the side of the large door. It would seem that this home was also used for the family's business dealings. How appropriate.

Having announced my arrival, Jacques returned and opened the door for my descent. I was not normally one for all these social etiquettes and protocol, but knowing that it was not only required but also strictly enforced by Jacques, I did my best to pay it no mind. As if I were not already aware, another clue was plainly laid before me that my life from here on out would not be of the same concord that I was accustomed to enduring. For, Atlas was trotting down the steps of the home—a smile plastered upon his face as he came to greet me on his very doorstep. Jacques' face twisted into a sour pinch, letting out a small grunt of disapproval at this break in etiquette, but he said nothing more. It was, in fact, quite a hilarious situation.

"It is so wonderful that you were able to make it, Thaddeus!" the human cheerfully exclaimed.

He wore quite opulent clothing today, with rich maroon hues and golden leaf accenting. It was a rather complementary color to his features, his eyes gleaming like opulent sapphire gems. I found myself laughing—the both of us shaking hands as if this were not a dubious ploy, but rather an actual attendance of friendship-building.

"Thank you for hosting, Atlas! Yes, your help with the planning of these events will be quite helpful, and I am looking forward to working with you." I kept it simple, nothing out of the ordinary for any present or hidden ears that may be listening.

As our greetings concluded, another carriage came upon the house, and I recognized it as one belonging to the Marquardt family. A servant emerged, riding on the back of the carriage. He wore the same sour expression on his face that Jacques seemed to have, but again nothing was said. The door was opened, and two faces peeked out from the shadow of the cart.

Atlas easily peeled from my side, walking up to the cart and offering a hand for stability. "So wonderful to see you, ladies. I have drinks and food available for your pleasure. I am so thankful you have come for us to plan."

Agatha stepped out of the carriage first, cloaked in black attire.

She took Atlas' arm and stepped gracefully down from the behemoth. I had more than an inkling that she did not care for the human, and I do believe it ran deeper than his finding out about the intimacy that she shared with Evelyn. Yet, to those around us or anyone looking, she was pleasant and took his arm, walking into the Charrons' home.

Evelyn did then emerge. Per usual, she wore very little color. Her brown eyes caught my own, and today she was much more confident—not a note of shamefulness to her demeanor. I offered my hand, and gently hers took hold of it. She smoothly stepped down and smiled.

"It is good to see you, Thaddeus," she pleasantly greeted.

I nodded my head, offering a kind one in return. "You, as well. Are you excited to begin the planning for our festivities?" I asked, trying my best to make seemingly natural conversation as we headed in.

"*Mmm*," she hummed and smiled sweetly as she looked up at me. "I am quite curious about the proposals that Atlas will have, as it seems he has quite a few."

I nodded in agreement. Entering the Charron home, I was left to wonder if his letters to the ladies contained more content.

Atlas led our company into the house and drawing room, prepared with food and drinks. It looked luxurious, as there was too much for only the four of us to lunch on. We followed Atlas' lead into the room, and he then promptly turned on his heel and closed the doors. He spoke out to—I assume—the shocked and displeased faces of our servants and entourages.

"We are more than capable of feeding ourselves, gentlemen. Feel free to stand and wait, or take lunch in the kitchens if you so desire," he happily chimed before locking the doors.

Atlas turned right back around, striding forward and taking a seat at the head of the table. He reached over, acquiring some pastries, cheese and meats.

"You must have some cream puffs, my dears. They are positively *divine*," he chirped, glancing up at our still-standing figures. Atlas gestured to the chairs around the banquet, popping a treat into his mouth, and lightly teased, "Come now, sit down. No need to be as serious as the three of you are now!"

We gingerly advanced, and I pulled out a seat for each lady. They sat next to one another, rounding the table, and I took my own seat to the right of Atlas. As the three of us faced him, the human reached over and took my hand, raising and kissing it. Immediately, my face exploded in an embarrassed blush. I was stuttering and trying to speak, but Atlas quickly did so with ease.

"It's wonderful to see you, my dears," he said and gave a satisfied smile, turning to the women.

"So you are a pair of mollies," Agatha accused, her eyes narrowing. Evelyn gave her a small elbow to the side, but Atlas was quick to our defense.

"And yourselves a couple of tribades!" he sniggered, continuing to hold my hand.

He propped his face up on bent arm, palm holding his chin with the other. Evelyn's pale face bloomed with a blush that rivaled mine, and Agatha clicked her tongue, eyes remaining lethally trained on her target.

The human chuckled again, brazenly continuing, "That's where we are at, darlings—two highly placed heirs of society forced into marriage by their families. From just my observation alone, neither of you desire such a matching, but they both have too much to fear from those families and too much respect for one another to let the other become a scapegoat...Then thrown into our mix," he paused and gestured to himself and Agatha, "a childhood love that continues to burn, and a budding endearment between two more recently acquainted lovebirds."

Atlas turned to me now—his blue eyes glimmering as he spoke the truth—raising my hand again and pressing it against his cheek. Evelyn's hand had also come up, crossing the tabletop to hold Agatha's. There was a longing ache in her eyes as she nodded at Atlas' words.

"It's true," her voice quivered, "but what can any of us do?"

At the grim's melancholic words, Agatha became less rigid, clasping the younger girl's hands. The love between the two women was apparent—powerful feelings that I now knew myself, though newer in its cultivation than their own. Against my hand, which was still pressed to Atlas' cheek, I felt as the human's grin turned up at the corners of his lips once again.

"Why, get married of course," Atlas purred. Immediately, Agatha's sour eyes were upon him, but he held a finger up to silence her. "Let me explain. For, what would any protest from either Thaddeus or Evelyn achieve? Nothing, spare perhaps a berating or beating! It's the very reason that both have been so respectful thus far and have been holding their tongues."

Evelyn's eyes and my own connected across the table, and we solemnly nodded in agreement. "Yes, Atlas, but what is your point?" I asked, urging him to get to the point. In that moment, it merely felt he was rubbing salt to the wounds.

"My point, dearest," Atlas chimed happily, "is to avoid the scandal, the catastrophe, Bedlam or the hangman's noose. If you two wed, why should that mean suddenly we cannot see our *truly* loved ones?" The trio of us blinked with a realization of where he was going. "You two," he gestured between Evelyn and myself, "marry. What next? You get your own house, apart from your fathers' brooding glares, right? Typically, you may go to live with Thaddeus' family for a time, Evelyn, but a house of your very own is on the horizon for the both of you." He then pointed to the table, silently tapping it thrice. "Right here, this gathering of friends is all that we need as a cover for seeing the person we truly long to be with. We can continue explaining it for now as festivities—planning for parties and such—but then it sets a precedent."

Agatha—more than the rest of us, I would go so far as to report—was astounded. She looked to Evelyn, squeezing her hands together above the table. "Th-This could work, Eve..." she liberally spoke.

Evelyn fervently nodded, her face colored pink with excitement—though it may also have been from the use of her nickname. She looked over to me with glowing optimism. "It could, could it not, Thaddeus?" she asked me.

Proud of his formulated plan, Atlas held his head up, grinning at me and my answer. "It's downright diabolically ingenious," I laughed, leaning forward and pressing my forehead against the human's.

Atlas held my head in place, nuzzling me and then looking back to the women. "There are a few bumps we will need to get over. Case in point," he stated to both pairs' current proximity to their chosen mate. "We will have to get used to this affection in each other's presence."

Agatha scoffed, wrapping an arm around Evelyn. The grim comfortably fell into the side of the witch, cuddling her lovingly. Upon Evelyn's face was the happiest smile I had ever seen from her.

"Do you really think I will be paying any attention to your

snogging faces, when I have my own belle?" she asked with a shot at us.

"Touché," Atlas responded with a smirk. He then continued, "Outside of your wedding day, no intimacy would be required between those betrothed, which really wouldn't be out of the ordinary. Many marriages are devoid of it thereafter...Surely, Agatha and I can keep cool heads about it. Do you think the two of you can refrain from falling in love at first kiss?"

I merely rolled my eyes, giving him a playful bump with my head. "I think we can manage that," I chuckled.

Holding his chin, I guided the human's face toward mine, leaning in and kissing him. It was long and drawn out—our first intimate and true kiss since the day we met. This was not a stolen moment, rushed and feverish so as to get enough to satisfy us until we would next meet. It was loving and perfect.

My anxieties leading up to this day were proven to be for naught. All of us seemed to finally breathe a sigh of relief, for we had a tentative plan for the future and that seemed enough. Our kiss broke, and Atlas clapped my arm, standing up and straightening his jacket.

Atlas exclaimed, "This has gone wonderfully, and with fewer attacks on me than I would have thought—I shall retrieve champagne to celebrate! Then we can discuss what you truly are here for...my ideas for your engagement masquerade party!"

His heels clicked as he gracefully left the room to procure a suitable drink from the cellar. We all cracked up in his wake, as celebration was overdue. The human had hardly left the room, however, when Evelyn spoke up from her cuddled position against the witch. Straightening herself up, her expression became worried.

"Thaddeus," she whispered, "we are beyond grateful for this

allowance. His proposition is as agreeable to us as it is you, but he..."

"He is mortal," Agatha was short and to the point. "With no supernatural ancestors, eventually he will realize that while he ages, you do not, and *we* just barely do." Her words, though harsh, were true. It was a truth I had been struggling with myself.

Evelyn hushed Agatha, leaning forward now with her hands folded on the table. She spoke, "Thaddeus, I understand that those of us who fall into this caste system love passionately, and our focus cannot be swayed. It is a heavy burden we both have felt, but today we have found a way to get through it and allow our hearts freedom." Agatha held Evelyn's hand as my bride-to-be continued speaking her mind, "In this agreement, I will allow whomever you request, but I urge you to practice caution with a human. Despite how delightful I do find Atlas..."

"Very few relations with mortals end with happily ever after," Agatha stated pointedly.

I nodded in understanding and clasped my hands in front of me, mirroring the grim's position. I tried to explain, "Although I am sure it's been said many a time before, Atlas is different." The pair sympathetically smiled at my words, but I continued, "He steals my very breath with how he moves—as if he too is not of mortality. He fears not what we have between us. I am confident that knowing such secrets of our world would be an absolute delight to him." I quietly laughed, nodding my head and looking between the women seriously. "He will know, sooner or later. I desire for the timing to be right, and I will expose myself and family alone. His reaction will dictate what the next steps would be, without endangering you both."

The pair seemed content with these circumstances for the time being, and Evelyn reached over to me, her hand upon mine. "Thank you for everything, Thaddeus...truly." Evelyn's gratefulness was apparent, yet a worried shadow lingered in her expression. "Though, I feel very much that you are the one who has most to lose with this arrangement. Again, I will urge caution, but nothing more."

I nodded to her, and although the worry lingered, for now this issue was not urgent to address. For my own sanity, I had to take the small victory we had achieved today. At the very least, did allow for a brighter future and possibility of happiness—and that was something to relish in. Finally, a spoon of sugar, the first positive step down a treacherous and tumultuous road.

Atlas soon returned with a bottle of champagne, graciously filling everyone's glasses. The air was much more relaxed now. Evelyn and Agatha curled up next to each other as they listened to Atlas boast of his grand plans for our engagement party. It was wonderfully soothing to be able to press my weight against the human, to touch him without fear or doubt.

I casually slung an arm around his frame, burying my face into his golden hair, my thoughts lingering on the very difference between him as a human and myself as a supernatural being. Getting lost in thought was a common practice in my youth. His words about plans for the party were lost on my ears. I could only focus on the movement of his golden hair and his very scent. In my soul—no, deeper—in my *bones,* I knew that this happiness was momentary. Clinging to ignorance, I ignored the building feeling.

Perhaps, if I had paid more attention, things could have been different.

CHAPTER 11

It had been concluded during the salon that our engagement party would be a masquerade ball—a particularly extravagant one, so as to waste my father's money. Atlas had invented this plan as a means for us to enjoy the night with our intended beloved.

Unbeknownst to the human, for our supernatural courts, a masquerade is almost always the route that is chosen for such events as this. Masks and costumes allowed free movement of our more natural selves, even in the presence of those who were mortal. Unnatural hair colors would be considered wigs, for instance, and so on and so forth. It was a pleasing trick to many in these hidden circles. Though, for simplicity, the trio did allow Atlas to maintain belief that this event was solely his idea. We were sent with dates to keep in mind and discuss with the heads of our families.

Given the conclusion made during the guised part of our meeting, we focused our attention mostly on our chosen mates. It is worth noting that creatures of supernatural status, in general terms, were not opposed to such situations as this, either. That being, the close proximity of pairs engaging in either romantic or sexual conversation, intimacy or acts.

It was somewhat common for covens or packs containing

more than one type of creature not to be related through famil-ial blood—but rather, they might be mated pairs or trios. There is strength in numbers, so having people upon whom you could trust and rely was always a factor. This was not something that humans did, which is why I was all the more surprised by how easily Atlas fell into such intimacies—considering how promiscuous and thus taboo it was to humanity. Our pairs sat together, embracing, speak-ing in hushed whispers and stealing soft kisses.

One advantage of our cunning plan—posing as close friend-ships—was that individual interaction would not be particularly frowned upon in the human society, especially for the ladies. The pair were already good friends, having been raised together with Agatha employed by the Marquardt family. To go on secret dates was not all that challenging for them, as generally women did ac-company other women on daily errands and shopping. Often, one would visit another to simply talk. They could enjoy gossip to-gether or even embroider before retiring for the night. There were plenty of opportunities for them.

From my experience, I assumed it would be less so for us gen-tlemen. Typically, the few times younger nobles and those of the merchant class intermingled was for business dealings. As afore-mentioned, Atlas' particular business was in exquisitely crafted car-riages. For such an exchange, one or a few dozen meetings could be called for, but for such meetings to continue indefinitely was not likely. It truly was a clever ploy, having the human as coordinator of our engagement festivities. Placing himself in such a role would require an ample amount of long, drawn out meetings, discussing every nuance of the party.

This would also give people the impression that we had be-come good friends, more so than a few business attendings would suggest. Planning such a party together could provide a more likely opportunity—being that we had become further acquainted—for a friendship to have blossomed. Therefore, it would make sense to regularly invite the heir merchant to further get-togethers.

All things considered, this moment of freedom was a wonderful treat. Always the one with most sense, however, it was Atlas who cleared his throat and turned his gazing affections from myself towards the women.

"Though we desire a longer time, we must not press our luck quite yet with two men and two women all alone. For who knows what scandalous rumors could begin from it?" With a simper, the human stood and offered his hand to the ladies, "I have more business with Thaddeus, discussing a wedding gift for his bride-to-be, but for now it would be best that we escort you to your carriages."

Wonders never ceasing on this day, Agatha and Evelyn stood. The witch took Atlas' hand and quipped, "You are a clever one. I will grant you that, sir—such a quality that could grow on me yet."

The witch turned to Evelyn, placing one last languid kiss on the younger's brow and then allowing Atlas to escort her from the room. Evelyn awaited my own arm, gently taking it when offered and walking alongside me. Her brown eyes shimmered, full of life at our new, devious charade. In our passing, quite the juxtaposition of servants and chaperones alike cast sideways glances and raised brows. As the carriages were drawn, we idly chatted. Atlas made a point to loudly state that we all should gather again soon to decide upon the colors for the wedding.

"Won't we have a wonderful amount to choose from in the coming weeks as winter wanes?" he happily chirped, gaining beaming smiles and a enchanted giggle from the bride-to-be. This sheep among the shrouded wolves was ever in his element with his title of grand marshal. With all his charm, Atlas bowed and kissed the hand of each lady as they clambered up into their landau. *"Adieu,"* he bid them farewell. Then we waved them off as the carriage clattered away.

We returned to the apartment, and doors were once again closed on servants' faces under the guise of an important gift from groom to bride that *must* be discussed. A faint click—which any mundane would not have heard—followed after the doors' closure. Atlas gestured for me to sit on the chaise longue tucked in the corner of the room as he topped off our flutes with more champagne.

My disguised eyes watched every movement, memorized every beautiful aspect of this man—how his hair bounced yet hung artistically around his face, the scent of his breath crossing his mortal lips. In this naive time, I was a silent soul, always calculating and evaluating in a brooding silence, internalizing my thoughts and observations. Only on the rarest of occasions did I ever voice such thoughts.

Ironically, this human was my near exact opposite in that aspect. Atlas turned, catching my staring trance, and gave a small sigh. Golden head shaking and clicking his tongue, the bottle was set down on the table, abandoned as he stepped forward.

"You look so very hungry, *mon chéri.*"

His blue, depthless eyes reflected a desire I felt pooling in my gut. A blush rose to my face, but our connected gaze remained as we were transfixed on one another. He stood above me, leaning down and brushing the hair from my face. His hand was gentle, holding my bangs back with a steady pressure that I allowed to tilt my head back, resting it upon the ridge of the lounge. I could hear the deafening rush of blood as my heartbeat quickened in my temples.

Yet, I heard each whispered word clearly as he spoke, "What is it that you desire?"

His heated gaze continued, lips hovering mere centimeters from mine. The burn of want clawed in my abdomen, making my mouth dry as a moan from the mere yearning for his contact threatened to dribble from my lips. I drew him close, hands raising from the knee of my trousers to explore the human's frustratingly covered body.

The blonde let out a small giggle and asked, "Well?"

I leaned in, my lips brushing his as his playful hold kept me from expressing my wish. He wanted a confession, and he easily was going to achieve his goal.

"I want *you*," I pleaded, my voice a breathless pant.

Atlas chuckled, pleased with my answer. His hand fluttered down the side of my face, cupping it as his thumb traced my bottom lip. A few loose strands of hair fell back into my face as it was tilted to the side. His rosy lips descended on my neck, lightly kissing my jugular, then the center of my throat, his tongue lightly flicking out and tasting my skin.

"How, my *belle?*" he hummed.

My whole body ached, nearly rigid from arousal. My hormones ran rampant, hunger building. The beast within me desired a turn, whispered every ruinous and delicious thought. Bearing witness to this onset of delirium, Atlas grounded me, hand pressing between my thighs.

"Yes!" I hurriedly whispered, admitting my desire and need as I squirmed for further contact.

This desire was quickly fulfilled, as I heard skilled hands undoing buttons. What followed was the small rush and sting of the chilled air on my thighs. The small grunt I would have voiced in response was silenced as Atlas captured my lips. Deft fingers massaged my thigh, a gloriously tortuous action, as it stoked the flames of need, yet kept them at bay. The kiss ended with him slowly nibbling on my bottom lip, his breath soft as the taste of his tongue danced and lingered.

"Then one must be *quiet*, be observant, learn...and above all else, enjoy..." He paused, playfully gazing down. He nuzzled the flesh of my neck, then fixed his eyes on mine as I felt his breath on my skin. "We can only proceed if those steps are followed...Can you do that for me?"

I bit my lip, fervently nodding to his question as a sign of good faith. Regardless of my intent, though, I gasped, writhed, and mewled wantonly under his loving caresses and kisses. A smirk was constant across his face, eyes beholding the gift before him with a small coo of curiosity.

When my thoughts drifted to certain parts of anatomy, I suddenly worried if Atlas would notice my nonhuman traits—be it the subtle differences of my body comparably to that of the mundane's, or any of the number of sounds I could produce that threatened to spill forth. Purring in particular came to mind in this moment, as I chewed on my bottom lip to prevent one from sounding in my chest. However, this amazing, stunning human paid no mind, nor did I give it further thought, as his tongue deviously flicked out, tracing along my skin. My eyes then fluttered closed, a quiver of pleasure dancing up my spine. He was intoxicating, addicting, and his overwhelming presence had me fearing overdose. It was hypnotic, and in my disheveled state I was a weak victim to his technique. When the euphoria faded, I could finally breathe once again.

"What do you think?" he chimed. He was charmingly cheeky. On a good day his attitude was a welcome challenge, and in this situation, it assisted my confidence. His appearance was much slenderer than my own. *Pretty* was an adequate description, *delicious*.

And I had every intent to have a taste.

CHAPTER 12

The cool, late summer gradually changed, as did the colors of the trees. Their leaves decayed from vibrant green to yellow, then to burnt orange and red. They disappeared with the sharp bite of winter winds—harsh bitter chills that breathed the land into a snow-covered wasteland.

In the cold days and weeks that followed our pact, all too many opportunities were presented for the four of us to congregate. Many transpired like the first, under the guise of party coordination. Eventually, those simply led to visits of a group of like-aged individuals. These meetings led through the holidays, and the most pressing event in discussion was my family's New Year's ball—which this year would additionally serve as our engagement party.

It was on all lips, discussed as the single most sought-after invitation for the celebration of the New Year. To my dearest Atlas should that be credited—as this celebration included an appeal of his own creation. The ball and engagement party was combined as a masquerade, and how the noble lords and ladies did covet such events.

A comfortable friendship was established between the four of us, even Agatha and my human. She did not care for him initially, but as he so swiftly had done with me—through small steps and persistence—Atlas gained her approval. This proved an unlikely alliance in the ball's planning, as there were secrets plotted between the two of them that only left Evelyn and me curious.

The group became more at ease with our dubious plot as it became an easy ruse to uphold. We found it, at times, all *too* easy a thing to accomplish despite our plentiful worries at the start. Double dates were our reliable default—for walks in the park, trips to the theatre, or for tea. It was a simple feat to sit with our actual mates, when the men and women were seated separately in the more intimate settings. On other occasions, we needed an actual turn system for who could rub shoulders with their partner that day.

Even between Evelyn and myself, a deeper friendship grew, as we did have to go on our own dates (a "critical element" to our ruse, Atlas would say). It was required, being that we were the candidates of marriage—the marriage of the season, no less. We found it to be not quite so terrifying of a thing, this strange future we were cultivating. Our individual dates often consisted of long talks, dreaming of the future. We quite liked the idea of having our own wing of the manor—away from her religious family and cunnings.

We also discussed the plan of Agatha staying on as Evelyn's lady in waiting—something I, of course, had no objection to. I planned upon entering into business, as an investor to Atlas' family affairs. Surely, that could allow almost daily meetings. However, Evelyn and I knew we could not escape the political sewage of my family for the first few years of our marriage, and we would live at the Avalone Manor. Still, the prospect of having our own home and domain was all too sweet of an idea not to fantasize about.

Soon came the eve prior to the masquerade, the grand event

that—although I and the city had heard so much about—during which I was finding I knew very little of what would transpire. Evelyn, as well, was left quite in the dark. Atlas and Agatha were easily conniving and capable of many mischievous surprises when their thoughts were combined, so I could only imagine what the following night would bring.

The hours did seem to lengthen through the evening before the event, though it was no different than any other. I ate alone, spare Jacques' attention and a footman serving my meal. Afterwards, I took a scotch and some lore to study beside the fire in the drawing room. Though often such texts could hold off my wandering thoughts by diving into their mysteries and tales, the excitement that bubbled up within me was proving inimical to any form of focus, and thus the minutes and hours crawled around the clock face.

Unable to focus upon the papers scattered before me, I stood up, walking over to the hearth and leaning against the mantle. An ironic chuckle managed to come up from my chest, shaking my head as I watched the fire's flames leap and devour the wood. While every year previous I had held contempt for this very party, now I could barely stay still from the excitement for the following evening. I heard the door open and turned my head—a pair of white wolf ears springing up in attention. Jacques stood in the doorway, a lax smile breaking out over his face as he entered the room.

"Good evening, Thaddeus," he greeted, not really giving me a spare moment to return the greeting as he stepped forward with a small box in his aged hand. He set the gift on the mantle and slid it towards me.

Managing to catch the small box, I looked to Jacques with a curious look. "What is this?" I asked, my amber eyes shining with curiosity and surprise.

Jacques let out a small *harrumph* to clear his throat and clasped his hands behind his back. He bowed his head slightly in apology for the informality, then spoke, "Surely, such a gift for your engagement to Lady Evelyn would not be appropriately given amongst those from your family and acquaintance, so I do ask your forgiveness, but I wish to give you mine now."

A warmhearted sigh left me, and I smiled back at Jacques. He had been by my side since my mother's passing—he was my teacher and guide through my budding life thus far. Though I was not immune to his sideways looks or the occasional reprimand in my youth, Jacques took pride in my education and his hand in my upbringing. Now, his fair eyes held a shimmer of fulfilment when cast upon me.

"I thank you, Jacques, for everything thus far and forward into my future," I stated, opening the small box. Tears were nearly brought to my eyes upon the sight of my gift.

"You are a man now, soon to be wed. As such, you are in need of the ring that will carry you through adulthood," Jacques softly spoke to me. His chest was puffed up, so proud of his creation. "The one you bear is not nearly as strong as it should be, leaving effort on your part to maintain your appearance with circumstances of higher stress. Your mother also had this difficulty when she came to live here..." He paused, no doubt because he had been so fond of her. It was not without difficulty that he continued to speak, "So from her final necklace, I created for you this band. Her name is Eikþyrnir."

Nestled in the box, lined with black velvet, was a grand silver circlet. The stones were the same as Garmr, as they had proven to be the most compatible with holding my mundane appearance. The main and largest stone—a garnet—was held in the antlers of two sparring stag heads, and below their mouths were two turquoise gems. This band was far from traditional, as the Avalone family crest was wolves, and the generations of elite breeding ensured wolves were one of the few forms they could change into. However, my mother and her people were quite different from their Old-World cousins. They could transform into a number of different animal skins and forms, averaging a half-dozen different shapes, though a handful were more comfortable to shift into. For my mother, one of those skins was a large white deer.

"She is beautiful," I finally managed to state, looking up from the gift and back to Jacques. "May I try her on?" I asked.

He nodded, and with a snap of his fingers produced a sizable mirror, held up for my use. "Should she be compatible and to your liking, you will need to wear her for the night so she can imprint upon you. Unlike Garmr, whichever first form you take with Eikþyrnir, she will remember. Upon putting her on for the first time, from then on, she will project that form onto you."

I nodded in understanding. Looking into the mirror, I focused on all the little details of my face, eyes fading from their vibrant amber hues to muddled brown circles like pits of roadside mud. With my teeth and ears smoothing out, I nodded to Jacques, and he set down the mirror. From the jewelry box he pulled out Eikþyrnir, sliding her onto my thumb. As the ring made contact with my skin, I felt a pleasant, pulsing sensation run up my arm. The feeling was as if my whole arm had been dipped into melted wax. It slowly burned up my shoulders, then down my spine in rapid succession. It was soothing—a testament to the power and compatibility I had with this ring.

"Wow..." I managed to mutter, an amazed laugh rising up from my chest as I turned back to the mirror. Everything was held perfectly in place, my form frozen as mundane. "With Garmr, it was always so...He was so *heavy*," I commented, formulating the English wording to try and describe just how different the magic felt between the two rings.

Jacques nodded and offered a rare genuine smile, which I only ever saw in my presence alone. "I am glad to hear this, young lord... If I may?" He asked for my hand to demonstrate. I extended my hand to rest in his as he used his pinky to point to her anatomy. "As you are aware, this is not your paternal crest, but rather a structure that holds resemblance to that of your mother's people," he began. "I have long observed you as your attendant, and your inheritance is stronger of her blood than your father's...Yes, his influence is apparent in your similar appearance..." he said, gesturing to my face. "But you were born from her, and her blood is your blood, Thaddeus. While you grew in her womb, her magic created and became yours."

Although I by no means had any expertise in the creation of these trinkets we used, I understood what he meant. "This ring bears the symbol of the blood my magic reflects and manifests as...and that creates a much stronger bond between myself and Eikþyrnir."

"Correct," he pointed to the band itself. "I melted down the silver of your mother's necklace, and while it was in that molten form, I laced it with a strand of her hair."

"Under the recent frost moon, I would assume?" I asked, gaining a chuckle from Jacques.

"So the young lord can retain my magic teachings," he teased, nodding to confirm my observation.

Crafting jewelry under a season's full moon helped to energize it—this was a skill that took a strong witch, capable of harnessing such power into a form that would not shatter or dull over time. In fact, this was one of the many reasons a powerful witch would be employed to larger households, as they were the only ones with the skill and ability to repair or create surrogate jewelries till the following moon.

"The instructions I received for when a charm needed to be created for you, Thaddeus, were to make them in the same template that we had followed for your father's family in past generations." He held my hand between both of his, his dark eyes catching mine. "All these years I have been by your side as you grew, Thaddeus. With each step you took, I could only be reminded of your mother and how very different her people were, how...they were, compared to the hegemonized breeding here..."

"I feel as if your words and the intention of this gift are going beyond just a warm reminiscence of my mother, Jacques," I observed.

He never was one to meddle, but Jacques did observe, absorb and occasionally state his thoughts to me. Many witches had a connection to the earthly elements and world surrounding that neither I nor any other supernatural being could hope to possess, which is what often led to their persecution. My only firsthand comparisons were Agatha and Jacques.

At my words, Jacques took pause, his hands pulling back from mine. "I have spoken out of turn, young lord. Please forgive me." He began to backpedal—typical fashion for this man—but tonight my piqued curiosity could not be brushed under the rug.

"Jacques," I said his name firmly, followed by a sigh of fondness. "As you just said, you have known me for the whole of my life." He puffed up slightly, perhaps to further ask for forgiveness or to bury what it was he had meant to say, but I quickly shot him a look that flattened his ruffled feathers. "You then *know* that surely I would take no offense to your observation, speculation, and thoughts on this matter, as I have had very little knowledge provided to me about my mother—simply faint memories and the few whispers I can manage to catch." I gestured to the remaining bottle of scotch and my still quarter-full glass on the table. "Please have a glass for yourself and top me off, as I very much wish to hear your thoughts on this."

Jacques released a small grumble but did as I requested of him. He collected a second glass, pouring himself a half portion and filling my own. I leaned against the fireplace mantle, collecting my glass and holding it up to Jacques with a nod for him to continue as I sipped the liquor. The witch huffed, throwing back his glass and nearly drinking his whole portion. With a small hiss, he sucked air between his teeth. His old eyes looked to the dancing flames of the fire, and they reflected the wild colors.

He began, "Everything on this side of our world—England, France, the whole of Europe—has been and *is* controlled so very carefully to protect any extramundane thing from being known by the vast populace of humankind. Thus it has been for all of mankind's history, for the mundane outnumber us, and with numbers comes the possibility of supernatural beasts being hunted down and wiped out. Always...always from the shadows have those who are not mundane lived and operated." He finally paused, looking at me. "There have always been families like the Avalones, made of alphas—their strength raising them to the head of the pack—but with their cunning and charm, they would hook their claws into governments and keep humans blind to us. Humans lived in ignorant bliss, and we could raise families. In this manner, all has been right with our world."

It seemed as though I had opened a vein of history and mystery from the head of Jacques. It was pleasing, his voice soothing and deep as he educated me, even though his words held ominous vapors that mixed with the scent of the burning birch in the hearth. I was reminded of stories he would tell at my bedside in my adolescence. Despite the gnawing worry that this narrative of his was turning to a more sinister verse, his baritone notes only kept me enthralled by his words and submerged in his yarn.

He inhaled a slow, trembled breath, accompanied by a shake of his head. "Then the Americas were found, Thaddeus. It was mysterious and new. I was among those elated of the discovery and eager to learn from it, but...the centuries of difference were apparent." His fist clenched against the mantle. "Supernatural beings were controlled here—arranged marriages chosen, and heritage decided for less desirable traits to be bred out.

"And when those of us from this side of the globe set foot on that land, many new beasts and beings were found, but we also found out what would have happened if the controlled and selective breeding had not been conducted." He leaned his forehead against his clenched fist on the mantle, watching the dancing flames as they sputtered and popped. "There are broad terms used, you know this. *Shifters* can refer to any werebeast, ranging from a mono-different skin like your fiancée to the most elite—such as your family, who specializes in a few different animal skins. Your *mother*, however, and her people were *more*."

"More?" My position mirrored his, arm braced on the fireplace mantel, but my eyes were locked on his face. This was no longer a bedtime story but rather a history lesson, the raw and real explanation of events.

"The breeding that your paternal family enforced has occurred so as to further guaranteed one's ability to hold a mundane form. However, over time this has limited their capacities..." His voice quieted, "Even your father can only shift to a large bear or a wolf, but your mother could change into anything she had ever laid her eyes on, and more."

"What do you mean by that?" My brow furrowed as I questioned him. Despite my question, I could see the pieces he was giving me fitting together like a puzzle—but the few final pieces had yet to fall from his lips to complete the picture.

"The indigenous peoples used the term *Skin Walker*, as you know, among the locals and tribes where your mother came from. The form of a large white deer with the fangs of a coyote came easiest to her. Though as for any new creature she came upon...She only had to take one look, and she could easily shift into its form. If her people's superiority was not apparent in that feat, then it became clear the night she transformed into a copy of your father."

It felt as if the air had been sucked from the room, from my very lungs. Hearing him say this, I was certain it was simply impossible. "No shifter can do that—"

"No shifter from *this* land could, Thaddeus," he persisted, "but each and every one of her people could do so. With ease, they could take any shape of any beast, man or animal. She once explained to me that if she could visualize how the muscles operated and moved, she could change into anything. Each one of her immediate kin could do this...Then very suddenly, they all disappeared, and only herself was left. *Then...*"

"Then only me?" I asked skeptically, following my words with a soft laugh. I outwardly did my best to remain cynical to his words, but I could not deny how my belly and mind burned in thought of the possibility. This twinge of familiarity was accompanied by a hollow and barren hole in my heart as nagging fear gripped my chest in its freezing grip. "As you have said, Jacques, you have known me for my whole life. Wouldn't you or I have noticed if I had such an inherited ability?" I asked.

What happened next, I could not have expected. Jacques' somber eyes pulled away from the flames of the fire, and the bottomless pools were the color of a storm-blackened sea. I saw the fear I felt in my chest reflected back to me. This fear was not towards me or what I was. The fear was *for* me, for what was in my blood and what that meant for me in the eyes of the paternal family who I was housed and fed by. I was not afraid of Jacques, nor do I believe he meant me harm, but the answer that hesitated on his tongue struck me with a cold chill.

"No one but myself has ever known the answer to that...and your mother's dying wish was that I would be the only one."

His hand reached out to me, holding the side of my face. The warmth of his magic melted into the skin of my cheek, and I felt as the waves of his magic pulled me under its waters. My eyes grew heavy. Having no way to resist as he pulled me into his arms, I fell unconscious.

His last words lingered in my ears, "It is time that you now know, Thaddeus."

CHAPTER 13

"Thaddeus...Where are you, little one?" An affectionate, genial voice called out to me.

There was a nothingness concealing me, embracing me—just that and the voice that called my name. I bathed in the sensation of safety and darkness, curling into a ball and letting it soak into my very bones. I had an awareness that I was dreaming, but...No, this was more than a dream. It was a memory—one long hidden, forgotten and now risen to the surface for me to experience again. There was a pull towards a woman's light voice, continuing to call for me. I held it at bay though, just a few moments more to feel myself sink in the black, depthless pool that surrounded me. I was in a sea of magic, and I knew it to be Jacques', both in color and weight. I wanted to feel as its embrace protected and held me. I could not stay as such, and the final lingering moment came. Bubbles lifted me up, rising me to the surface of this liquid magic, as a picture came into view.

Suddenly there was light, cast from a window as a great woolen blanket was pulled off of me. A woman with wild white hair hanging in tangled curls around her face giggled in delight of finding me. A pair of white canine ears perked up through her ferocious curls, magnificent antlers curling from her scalp as well. Her skin was pale, with rouged cheeks that made her amber-colored eyes gleam in the morning sun. A loving smile was breaking across her beautiful face, showing a pair of double canines.

"I have found you!" It was her voice, the one I had heard in the thermal waters, and it was dripping with honey and the heat of summer.

I squealed as she tumbled into the bed, with her fingers going to my ribs and drawing more squeals of laughter from my petite frame. She wore a thin cotton chemise that clung to her supple body. Actually, I wore one as well, so we must have recently awakened for the day. Her arms wrapped around me, and I felt peace and safety within them.

Her own light tittering rang through the air like chimes on the wind. Her plump, red lips pressed to the top of my unruly, white head. She let out a soft, warm sigh, inhaling my scent as we lay cuddled close, her honey-colored eyes closing. Again, her motherly embrace held me, and I felt tranquility, protection. The scent of her skin danced into my nose, and I remembered how she smelled of autumn air and browning sugar. I was so very aware that this was a memory, and I let it cradle me as she so lovingy did in those days.

Another kiss was pressed to the top of my scalp. A gentle giggle followed before her voice whispered to me, "How about we go down to the garden and run, my little pup?" Her words made excitement flutter in my boyish heart, a beaming, bright grin splitting across my face. In her eyes, I saw my reflection as a pair of snow-white wolf ears perked up against my skull, and a howl of thrill passed from my smiling lips.

"Yes, Mama!" I heard my own juvenile voice jingle on the air.

She excitedly pulled us from the bed, our bare feet padding against the hardwood cherry floors.

Quick and quiet, we left the room, sneaking down the hall nearly silently except for our muffled giggles. She would pause at each corner, glancing around them before then trotting forward. She picked me up when we came to the stairs, the pair of us giggling, though she sweetly shushed me. One of her hands was on the intricately detailed railing, the other holding me to her as she hurriedly stepped down. At the base of the stairs she turned, heading for the back rooms of the manor.

Passing through the manor's halls with great care, she aimed for the kitchen or servants quarters. Where my own tiny feet made hollow little thumps on the floors, she moved on her tiptoes, making not a sound. The final threshold approached, and she bounded through the doorframe. Though silent she had been, she stopped short. The decision she had made to slip out through the kitchens did not account for the fact that the cook was the first to rise in this home, and she now stood between us and the outside.

The cook was a stout woman with frizzy, wild red hair poking out from under the fabric that held it back. Her old, worn face looked up from the floured table, hands kneading a ball of dough. My mother held me close, as if hiding me for fear that I would be snatched from her breast by the woman. For her part, the cook's grey eyes sized my mother up, raising a red brow. Neither moved a muscle, eyes locked as the seconds passed.

Finally, the woman nodded her head towards the open door, smirking and winking to me before her attention fell back to the dough she worked on. "Breakfast will be ready in another hour, m'lady. Best if you are found back in your rooms then," the stout woman warned.

A wide grin spread across my mother's face, offering a slight bow of her head in thanks to the cook, and with a few more steps we bounded out of the back door.

It was an early fall morning. As soon as we stepped outside, the crisp air filled our lungs, and it was rejuvenating. There was a light fog, with dew on the grass that clung to my mother's ankles and the edge of her sleeping clothes as she walked towards the gardens. Despite the light chill, it felt wonderful to us both. Our temperatures ran hot, and we all too often wore stuffy clothes, which provided a constant miserable state during the daytime.

My mother pulled me from her breast and set me down in the grass, which earned a blissful giggle from me. I glanced up at her, as she did down to me, smiling in love and adoration. "Let us run, my darling boy. See if you can beat me to the middle of the gardens," she challenged, turning from me and beginning to sprint.

A shriek of enthusiasm burst from me as I toddled after her, my little legs pumping to carry me forward. As the distance between us widened, my spine tingled with a burning sensation. I could hear the rush and torrent of blood in my ears, each muscle throbbing as they seemed to contract and expand all at once in my little body. Before my eyes, I watched as my mother jumped in the air, her body morphing into a large white stag with tall antlers.

She landed on all fours, glowing amber eyes turning back to me as her chemise fluttered down from the air and settled onto the dew-dampened earth. She shook out each limb, stretching and letting out a small snuffle. She grinned, showing a mouthful of sharp pointed teeth, waiting for me to transform as well.

In my adolescence, I was not nearly as graceful as my mother, who was nearly one hundred years old. Regardless, a surge of white-hot energy burned in my chest, spreading to every inch of my body.

My skin split and regrew, fur sprouting on each patch of skin and hands turning to claws. My sleeping clothes were shredded as I took the form of a small wolf pup. Shaking out every limb with an excited wiggle, I felt the adrenaline of taking another shape coursing through my veins. I yelped eagerly, bounding and weaving between my mother's legs as we trotted into the maze of the garden.

It can be difficult to describe the sensation of changing forms, because not every time is it caused by the same reason, nor does it feel the same as the prior transformation. On this morning, it filled our bodies with a unique feeling—a mixture of adrenaline and euphoria, which blossomed throughout my whole body with small explosions of exhilaration. In this form, I could smell every flower that bloomed in the gardens, hear every critter that took cover as we passed. It was all too much and yet not enough simultaneously.

My mother let out a pleasant chuckle, nuzzling me and then raising her head. She quickened her pace, pulling away from me. It was turning into a game of tag, and I eagerly chased after my mother, jaw nipping at her heels. She stayed just out of my reach, jumping vertically, darting under a bush or around a tree. We played this game deep into the garden, to the secluded area that has set the scene more than once in this story of my life.

I rounded the corner, stopping short as my mother transformed back to her most comfortable form, which I did find to be the most breathtaking. Her long, untamed white hair held length down to her posterior. Upon her skin was a layer of dense white fur, from her neck down to her toes. Every inch of her private parts appeared as downy velvet under the morning sun. On her back were subtle brown spots, like that of a fawn. Though the tail that sprouted from the small of her back was long and thin—comparable to a lion's—it was nearly thrice that in length. Once more, a large crown of antlers sprouted forth from her skull, and those too were covered in velvet.

Her golden-eyed gaze turned downward, smiling love for me, her offspring. She nodded to me, encouraging me to transform as well to a bipedal form as she sat down upon the fountain edge. I sat in my wolf form, a small pout no doubt upon my face. My mother was beautiful, and the difference between us when she was in her default form upset me. I did not look as she did, and for that I cursed and blamed my mixed blood.

"Just try, my child," her silken voice encouraged, nodding to me again.

A small chuffing noise left me, and I closed my eyes. This transformation back into a state of homeostasis was entirely different than shifting into the skin of another beast. Instinctually, I knew I must relax, must calm every nerve that was alive and firing in order to keep the current form I held. Slowly, the endorphins and adrenaline siphoned off and were replaced with oxytocin. I focused on breathing deeply and letting a wave of calm wash over me. Also, I wished to take a form similar to my mother's. Even at such a young age, I wanted to be nothing like my father. Instead, I wanted to be as winsome and powerful as my mother was. At this age, brought to light in this memory, I knew that she was more, and I admired every facet of her being.

An excited intake of breath caused my eyes to open, and I saw my mother leaning towards me with an enthusiastic glimmer in her eyes. "Oh, my dear child!" she squealed in glee, hands together like a prayer, then holding her face. With her feet dancing happily, she patted the edge of the fountain next to herself. "Come look, my little pup!" she chirped gleefully.

I got up, supported by two little feet that were coated in a faint dusting of white fur. With wide-eyed wonder I looked at my arms, and the same dense white fur that covered my mother was now on every inch of me. I nearly tripped over my own feet, dashing forward to the fountain to look at my reflection. It was a near exact match to my mother's form, my own age or mixed blood causing but a few minute differences.

I did not have antlers like hers, but rather small nubs that were still buried under the skin. I only discovered they were there as I ran my hands up through my wild white hair, giggling happily as I pirouetted in place. My ears were like that of a wolf, large and pointed, whereas hers were cervine and parallel. Lastly, my tail comparably was shorter than my mother's. Where hers could wrap around her waist nearly twice, mine would barely do so once, though in appearance they were the same.

Her nurturing, loving arms wrapped around me, admiring our reflection and our matching qualities. "Oh Thaddeus, my dear sweet boy." She pressed kisses to my brow and temple and pulled me into her lap. My mother whispered loving praises to me, "I knew you would be more like me! I just knew it, my dear sweet child. Deep in my heart, I had never given up hope." I loved hearing her say such words, and how her maternal affections encased my small body like a delicate fabric as she held me.

She tilted my head up delicately, a mixture of happiness and intrigue upon her features. "Do you want to try one more trick? See how much like Mummy you can be, my little pup?" she asked. A desire to do so bubbled up inside of me, and I nodded my head. I wanted to see her mirthful. It was the same desire every child sought, to see their mother pleased with them, and that burned brightly within me. She mirrored my head nodding, and an adoring smile split across her face.

"Watch me, little one. Watch and listen." She pointed to her face and closed her eyes, her soft white lashes pressing to her cheeks. "Whoever you are changing into, you must imagine that every inch of yourself is changing into them, Thaddeus. Whatever emotion toward them you harbor—whichever is strongest—you focus upon it and let it flourish like wildfire in your bones. Focus first on their eyes..." Her own opened, and I blinked in confusion, nearly recoiling from her at first. Instead of her honey-hued eyes, reflected back to me were my father's dark, gelid ones. My first harsh instinct to recoil, though, quickly simmered as her mellow voice continued to walk me through the explanation of her process.

I have never experienced a love towards my father, for many reasons. The cultivation began while a babe for my heart to belong to my mother entirely. So despite her transformation into the one being who I felt the most fear towards, it was her voice and scent that kept me in a hypnotized state. As that fear was displaced, I could focus on what it was she was saying—this great secret she was demonstrating to me. It was like nothing my juvenile eyes had seen, as her fresh face was replaced with the aged-lined skin of my father.

Elation rushed through my young mind. Although my knowledge was limited to extended family, I knew no one could do what it was my mother now displayed. It was as if I were looking at a portrait of my father, and with hesitation, I reached my small hand up. My mother laughed, her still loving gaze fixed on me, and leaned into my outstretched hand. She cleared her throat, surprising me once again as she spoke. Like a parrot, her voice came out rough—and though not nearly exact, her attempt to mimic my father was sufficient enough that short phrases were inseparable.

"With time and practice, you can do this too, Thaddeus. We are the only two who can..." She cleared her throat, another giggle rising up from within her. Once again, I heard her sweet soprano tone. "However, my dear boy, you must keep this secret from anyone else."

As she spoke, this memory began to fade. I could feel the tropical clutches of the nothingness that had embraced me before this episode reaching out and trying to drag me back within its protective grasp. Her words grew more faint, reaching my ears through a veil, as if my head were submerged below water. I fought against this previously comforting hold, for it was hiding a very important truth. I could not submit as I wanted to prior—to cease existing in the depthless nothing. The scene that played out before me was too significant.

It reminded me of who I was—my mother's child. A piece of the puzzle to who I was, *what* I was, was locked carefully away in the one place it could be safe from any other. In my memory. It was left here by my mother for me to find again one day. So I reached out my small, thin hand to hold my mother's face, desperately trying to hear her words and stay within this memory. I needed to know what it was that I had forgotten.

"Only ever...Jacques...my dear, sweet boy...Don't let them— *HIM*—have it..."

Her head abruptly turned from me, and I felt myself sinking away from this evocation and rising to consciousness. The bubbles rising around me told me where the surface was, and I was nearing it. I could not breathe, for fear that if I did, the scene before me might fade into nothing as any dream would. I separated from my juvenile self, viewing the scene now as a spectator.

"Run!" My mother's voice rang like loud cathedral bells in resonating notes. I sprang from her arms and ran away into the gardens, and she rose proudly to her feet, facing the opposite direction. We both must have heard footsteps—or shouting, a name had been called—something that would expose this secret or ourselves. Why? Who need we hide from on our own lands? Why did she send me from her side to face this alone?

A foreboding shadow rounded the entrance to the fountain, but my mother's face did not change in time. He must have seen her. *He?* It was too faint to hear now...I was sinking and rising away. Who was it?

He grabbed my mother by the neck. She didn't fight him. Why wasn't she fighting him? His hand was crushing her throat.

"Lilît!"

Unable to withstand the paralysis of the nothingness, I was consumed. This memory went dark, my father's voice echoing coldly.

CHAPTER 14

I was aware that I was waking and dancing on the edges of consciousness from a deep, dreamed memory. The scene of my
mother being choked was burned into the back of my eyelids. My
eyes fought to open with the greatest effort, to look away from the
bone-chilling picture. Rolling around, my vision sought to focus
on anything in the space surrounding me. Coming off this dose of
magic—which I shortly deduced as culprit to my dreamed recollection—was a difficult undertaking. The ability to have opened
my eyes was nothing short of dumb luck, as such magic typically
incapacitated the recipient.

As my eyes rolled about the room, I took notice of my where-
abouts. I was bundled up and safe in my own bed, my own night
clothes. As my eyes shifted to the side, I saw a figure propped up
near the wall next to my bedside. It was Jacques, collar loosened
and slumped over, asleep. The whole picture was coming together. Since I was coming off this magical exposure and incapable of
movement, I took a pause to review my situation.

Magic involving one's memories in any form—be it recollection
or suppression—is a carefully executed skill. Steeping such an important organ as the brain in magic was an often temperamental and

thus unpredictable essence. Therefore, is a delicate matter, to say the least. For the safety of the recipient of such an intricate craft, it is cast in such a way that it immobilizes you, hence my predicament. Movement would come back eventually, especially given that the more frequently one is subjected to such magic—as is common across the board with other spells or hexes—the recovery time is lessened.

That being so, it brought me to my next thought. Perhaps the aforementioned ability to open my eyes was not dumb luck. I was managing, albeit weakly, to twitch my left foot under the sheets. Physically, I had experienced this magic before—likely in the suppression of those tortured memories that were still burned in my mind. I sighed, for despite just now waking, I was exhausted from this experience. So many questions lay on my numb tongue, pressing against my teeth to sound their pleas.

My amber irises fell back onto Jacques, watching him sleep in the soft morning light as my limbs awakened and my mind continued running rampant. He had kept this secret of my lineage for so long, perhaps longer than needed, but something had prompted him to show his hand to me. A chill ran down my spine as the last scenes of the memory flashed across my vision once more—the piercing tone of my father's voice resonating in my skull as his foul claws snuffed out my mother's life.

The very scene was a gut-wrenching reveal, for I knew now, undoubtedly, that she had been murdered. It was a hushed subject never to be speculated aloud, but an element of foul play had always been a likely possibility in my mind. With these unlocked memories, missing information was piecing together the whole picture of my history. My mother had not gotten sick and simply succumbed. It was my father's unloving hands wrapped tightly around her throat that ended her life.

How hard it must have been for Jacques. He held such endearment towards my mother and great affection for myself, and yet he had to live with knowing how she came to her end. Justice was but a vacant and hollow thought. Sadly, I cannot say that in these paralyzed moments I felt any grief. She was distant and far away now, and knowing these new truths only added further sadness regarding the tale itself, but not my emotional involvement.

What I did feel was a gnawing fear, breathing its foul breath against my neck. Why did Jacques feel that now was the time for me to know this? Jacques was a calculated man, and revealing these memories surely could not have been an easy decision. The alternative was to simply let these forgotten memories remain locked away—where Jacques himself had concealed them in my mind—along with the hanging doom and pain they bore. Why now? This was one of many questions I had for Jacques' soon to be awake ears.

Lilit. That was the name my father had hissed to my mother, but did he mean *Lilith*? As in, the first wife of Adam? That wasn't my mother's name, and I could not recall her ever being addressed as such by my father, nor by any other. Her Anglo name, Josephine, was chosen by my father, and from that day forward she had borne it with...almost pride, as far as I knew. Though, recent events led me to question the difference between what I remembered versus what was actual fact, and the burning itch remained that this usage of name held relevance. Then again, this episode of enlightenment showed me many things I had *not* known of my mother—and ultimately myself. I now recalled the form she had taken, the warnings she whispered to me.

I managed a wobble of my head, the movement enough so that my eyes could slip down to my hand. Upon my thumb, Eikþyrnir rested, keeping my form mundane as she hugged my skin and bonded to me. With her nestled on my thumb, I could not test what had happened in the episode. Once more left with increasing frustration, I was forced to simply lie with my thoughts.

"My mother was simply more." This quietly whispered mantra had often run through my thoughts. Hell, anyone who would ever speak of her would say it was so. Jacques was merely the latest, having done so last night, and now the rumination simmered again, fueled by these new facts of her. They were not just referencing the creature that she was or her differences to her Old-World counterparts—which, yes, were unique and mystical but not what they meant. As otherworldly as non-mundane creatures could be, she was on a level above the rest, and I just couldn't grasp why.

My eyes turned back to Jacques and burned into his sleeping form, trying to silently will him to wakefulness. All the things that reanimated—my foot, a few muscles of my neck—were absolutely useless to me. I needed him to wake and undo my state. Shockingly, with a paralyzed tongue and numbed lips, I was managing to make some syllables of sounds. A few grunting noises were better than nothing, so I tried again, this time with as much breath as I could muster. *"Wa...wak..."* I garbled out, and finally some luck was on my side. Jacques' eyes popped open, and he sprung to my side.

"Young lord—oh, yes. Here, let me help you up..." He quickly unbuttoned his sleeves and rolled them up to his elbows. Then, sliding his hands and arms under me, Jacques helped to lift me into a feeble but serviceable sitting position. "How are you feeling? It can be rough coming out of..." His eyes caught my own—unamused and obviously glaring—and in response, a very sad smile came upon his face.

"I know you have questions, Thaddeus, but it will be sometime yet before you can ask me...You should be up and about by this evening." He cleared his throat and went back, thankfully, to the more pressing subject at hand, knowing quite well that being able-bodied by tonight was simply not the most important discussion to be had. "Maybe I can tell you most of what I know to be true, and from there you should be able to ask your questions?"

In this moment, with the first morning light shining on his very sad face, Jacques also appeared as if a weight was being lifted from him. Finally, he was able to tell me that which he harbored for most of my life.

I let out a grumbling sigh, not yet capable of much more due to the magic paralysis. I rolled my eyes about the room before looking back to Jacques, as there was not much I could do to stop him. Even with this as my reaction, the lingering feeling that his next confession would hold those last pieces of the story burned in my belly.

"Thaddeus, I must start by disclosing...F-for your protection, I have not been entirely honest," he began. Unlike last night's sermon, he could not meet my line of sight. Jacques sat in his chair, arms upon his knees as he hung his head. "I suppose I had hoped you would remember, somehow, that you might overcome what my magic had hidden from you—even though I knew that possibility was futile." With trembling breath, he reached a hand to mine, for now he would show me what he knew.

Magic consumed my vision, showing Jacques' point of view while his voice echoed narration. A bonny, petite woman was pictured. Her white hair was voluminously wild and untamed, the length down to almost her knees. She was naked but covered in a layer of soft velveteen-like white fur, and on her head was a crown of antlers—every feature, in fact, the same as my memory. Pictured was my mother. In particular, she appeared how Jacques had first met her prior to colonization. Feral, beautiful and free.

"I met your mother when she was not much older than yourself. Practically a child by her people's standards. With my age, I can—I *did*—explore this world in ways no one else could, so I knew of the Old World, and I knew of the New. I simply kept watch and studied over each, but I interfered with neither."

The scene slightly changed. Now my mother was older, physically more mature. These scenes displayed as if hand-drawn, illustrations that flitted into view as he spoke. In one, she was surrounded by her people, who all resembled her with their skinwalker characteristics. In another, she ate at the head of a table, again surrounded by her people. She was revered, loved. In another scene, this time she lay out in the sun—upon the ground in a wooded area, her face nuzzled against Jacques' legs while she gazed at him.

"In one way, it was the same there as it is here. Much like your father's pedigree, an alpha female was precious, rare and to be cherished—and she was. Your mother was born as heir apparent, and though she took on her role at a young age, it was something she was born to do and did well. Her people were nomadic, and they migrated with the seasons. Given that they never stayed in a place for long, the supernatural peoples who were established in the areas they passed through came to view them as otherworldly benevolent beings."

One more picture sketched into my view. It was my mother, wrapped in a simple fabric, holding out her hand to a lycan child at her feet. She slowly helped the child to stand, and like the turning pages of a book, I watched as she led the boy back to the outskirts of his village. I realized that he had been lost in the woods, and she returned him.

"As I, yourself, and other people have whispered, she just was something more...It was after this, returning a lost child back to his family, that this thought became synonymous with thinking of her. Reason being, the other creatures began to revere her, and that transformed who she actually was. It was small at first..."

The drawn pictures were now of baskets—some containing gathered herbs, others bearing pelts or jewelry. "Offerings were first of thanks, but as decades of this continued, little by little, it turned to ritual and transformed into worship. That kind of devotion grants immense power to the recipient, and your mother was that recipient."

Another series of sketches flipped like the pages in a book. They showed years in only a moment—of my mother and her generosity, the compassion she had and how that affected the cycle of dependency between herself and the people who worshiped her. She collected these offerings and shared them with her own people. In exchange, predators who wandered too close would be found dead for the village to harvest. Livestock which got loose would be returned unscathed. She delivered warnings of dangerous weather, which packs could then prepare for.

"Round and round this cycle continued, and your mother only became *more*. The *more* that she became, was a god."

My vision cleared, and once again I was back in my room, lying in bed. Jacques sat beside me in the same head-hung position on his chair, not making eye contact. It was as if only a minute had passed, for the rays of the sun cast into the room had not changed at all. I also felt more in control of my body, the dead weight of my limbs fading. I could sit up a bit more, and I did—a hand reaching out to Jacques and taking his.

"You're telling me...my mother was a god?" I asked, my voice holding a heavy amount of skepticism, but even as I said it, *it made sense.*

"She had become one," he confirmed. "The technical classification, I suppose, would be a minor god, for she was not capable of great miracles, nor could she create great disasters of nature. From the power of worship, though, an omnipotent magic manifested in her. Its capabilities are comparable to that of, say, a witch—an old, powerful witch." He tried to put it into perspective for me.

As this new information settled in, some questions were answered, while others remained and even a few birthed anew. All my musings were a variation of *why?* "I...ah..." I laughed, my hand falling to my lap as I struggled to accept these truths and phrase my questions. "I'm at a loss, Jacques...Why call her Lîlît?"

That same, very sad smile remained upon his lips and broke wider yet across his face. "Oh Thaddeus, she was an amazing creature," he praised, apparently intending to answer my questions in his typical raconteur fashion. "The name was but a cruel nickname. You have to understand...Being elevated to the status of a god, abilities were gifted to her. Some of these abilities were in her control, and some were simply a symptom of what she was."

His hands quickly jumped up, like a conductor of a symphony, gesturing grandly as he continued, "The earth—the very *soil* where she and her peoples migrated—was rich and *full* of life, bountiful in both game and crops. Along with this came *peace,* an easy and quiet peace in the lands where she lived or passed through." He sighed lightly in remembrance. "When that peace, their utopia, was threatened, she offered herself up as a martyr for the slimmest hope that it could be maintained."

This rang true, given her humble and kind ways. Of course, she was like this with me, her blood and child. It also extended to staff, the livestock, and even to the flowers of the garden, or the butterflies that enjoyed it. Her soul was purer than I had even envisioned.

Jacques continued, "She traveled to the other side of the world and entered into a marriage with your father, thinking it would bring protection to her people."

"But it did not," I finished his sentence, my heart weighted. Horrid was the reality, as was how indisputably I knew it. Never talked about were those cousins from across the sea, which could only have meant they no longer existed.

"It did not," he repeated, nodding somberly. "They were slaughtered minutes after the boat carrying your mother left the bay, on your father's orders."

The breath was stolen from my lungs—my body flooded with anger, sadness and terror. None of these emotions were given the chance to completely seep in and take hold of my heavy heart before Jacques was again giving account.

"It was not lost on your father how special your mother was. The potential he saw to use her as a weapon is truly the only reason she had been allowed to live." His voice quavered, breaking as he held back a sob, "Had I known of her people's fate sooner... Despite having never interfered before...I-I would have *warned* her." He took a pause, cleared his throat and lifted his sleeve to dry the corner of his eyes. "In shadow, I boarded that ship, curious to where your mother's path would lead and what would come of this meeting."

My blood ran cold, every hair on my body standing on end at Jacques' recital. I wanted to banish the painful horror in my heart, as I knew how this story ended—with my mother's murder. Silently, I felt as my own tears welled up, blurring my vision before spilling over onto my cheeks.

After taking a moment to collect himself, with a trembling lip, Jacques continued. "Seeing it as her duty, she married your father and endured his cruelty under those false vows. She was bound to the estate, for a number of reasons. Especially in those early days, her appearance was not easily controlled. As a result of her presence, as seen by her nomadic wanderings before, the estate flourished. The gardens, crops, livestock—all of it was bountiful and unprecedented in its successful harvests. I applied and took on the role as your mother's personal retainer. A secret of our own was that we knew of each other prior to her marriage, which helped the relationship, though I don't believe anyone ever caught on."

I can only assume they never had, as here he was before me, still employed as my own. His emotions overcame him again, and unable to meet my gaze, his own tears fell into his lap.

"I confess it was for selfish reasons, Thaddeus. I wanted to closely watch the situation out of curiosity. Every day, though, it seemed just a little more desire for life would leave her, and with it came the slow breaking of my heart. Even one as radiant as she was, gradually was being milled down from the abuses she endured in this wretched place." He smiled then—inappropriate, given the melancholy subject—but a moment later I understood. "By some *miracle,* of which I will not speculate upon...she became pregnant with you."

His words, warm and kind at my mention, only held heartache for me. Despite the torment that every day held for her—the abuses which I could only fathom were worse than my own—still she had loved and cherished me, I knew. I missed her, I wanted to apologize for her suffering and to hold her. Never could I, and this hurt more than any cruelty I had known before.

"She fell in love with you before you were even in this world, her life once again brightening with each day that brought your birth closer. Your father's torment, cruel inquiries and experiments lessened as well. *Never* will I defend him," he hissed through gritted teeth, "but you were of his blood, so he spared her during the pregnancy." A disdainful sigh escaped him, and I could see anger simmering under the surface of his emotion. "Then the rumors began. It was near the end of your parents' fifth year of marriage when you were born. During that period of time, with regard to your mother, his...cruelty in general lessened. This continued after your birth and into your first year of life.

"Of the dry wagging of tongues, what I found actually to be truthful was little. It slowly became evident that your father didn't just want to use your mother as a weapon. Rather, he sought to *take* what she had for himself. However, my thinking is that he discovered it wasn't possible for him. This all happened prior to your birth, and so...Maybe it was that he lost interest—truly, only the gods know. Whatever the case, to others in the hierarchy, he was appearing soft." A dry chuckle rose up from Jacques at the thought. "On the other side of that, the more ecclesiastical creatures of this district speculated that she was bewitching him, and they came to see her as a false god—a *Lilit*. Many falsely proclaimed that she intended to try and take claim as alpha. I suspect these rumors played into your mother's fate."

Jacques raised his head finally, his recount seeming to have aged him years. In the time he had been speaking, his heartbreak became evident. "It is my belief that your father simply cut his losses and murdered your mother to silence those rumors."

CHAPTER 15

The remainder of the morning—the time leading up to the evening's event—seemed to pass by in a blur. I, myself, was simply numb to it all, not that my hand was needed in any of it. Servants and those hired for the event had been given their instructions and duties well in advance. I suppose after the avalanche of information befell me, I had eaten once and likely again later, and had been dressed by Jacques before he needed to leave me for his own masquerade duties. I did not remember much of any of it.

I could vaguely recall the weather being more than pleasant. The sun was out, melting the first layers of frost upon the grass. Only managing to recall this when I finally broke through my stupor, I found myself in the depths of my mother's garden. Sat upon her fountain's edge, I watched the daylight fading without much more than simple lounging attire on. I turned to look up at the marble sculpture of my mother.

Ominous and cold she now appeared, with her beautiful form reaching up into the sky. My throat burned, wishing again for such knowledge of her untimely end to be gone from my mind. My very soul ached, full of sorrow for her and the fate she met. I very well may have spent the remaining time intended for preparation and dressing in my depression, haunting the gardens well into the night, if not for a comforting hand that slid onto my shoulder.

"After all the work Agatha and myself have put into this party, you don't think I am going to let you sulk off on your own, do you?" Atlas' tender voice purred into my ear.

I turned to look up as the human sat down next to me. He had the beginnings of makeup dusting his face, smiling with a slight tilt to his head. Though remaining was indeed a seed of ache and woe, I could feel the tight grip of dejection loosening as my eyes beheld my human. His bright blue eyes seemed to sparkle at the sight of me. I could not hold back from such a state of joy, as he truly had a contagious atmosphere.

I didn't speak at first, leaning against Atlas and nuzzling my face against his. He inaudibly laughed, blonde curls bouncing lightly against my skin as he used his nose to tip my face upward, capturing my lips. He smelled like honey, lips tasting of cinnamon and cream. I felt the last of my dread melt away, if only for a moment, managing to return his smile as our lips parted.

"Of course not. I just...learned of some difficult news today..." My eyes cast up to the figure of my mother. I confessed with a sigh, "And I am missing my mother quite terribly."

Atlas' hand slid to the side of my face, gently stroking the lobe of my ear before pulling me in for another tender kiss. It was light, and regretfully not as lingering as the first. "Let it all fall away this evening, my dear. I will have you tell me later, but as for now, I want nothing more than for you to be merry and enjoy yourself. This party is for you...in *part*." He encouraged with a giggle, his eyes closed as a grin split across his face.

An exhale followed a nod, and then I smiled, standing up. "Yes, I can do that," I assured.

Atlas stood as well, and I pulled him close. Everything—ranging from the new information I was still digesting, to my life in general—seemed bearable when Atlas was with me, and especially when I could hold him in my arms.

"Good!" Atlas hummed with another quiet chirr, wrapping his arms around me and giving me a squeeze. "Then go get ready before *all* your guests have arrived and gone. We are going to have fun tonight!" he cheered.

Leaving the labyrinth, we parted ways. As grand marshal of the event, Atlas had many happenings and more than a few near-disasters to address. All were quickly paraphrased before he left my side, shouting to one of the many caterers. I was instructed to return to my rooms and dress in the costume waiting for me.

In this last hour prior to guests arriving, the whole estate was abuzz, showing more life than I could ever recall it having held before. Servants of the home, caterers, decorators and entertainment all fluttered around, working on the finishing touches. As I approached the building, every room seemed to have a candle alight in their numerous windows, casting a golden glow into the waning night sky and onto the lawn. It was ravishing, loud, and this created a joyous atmosphere. Only Atlas could have achieved this in a place of such secrecy and death.

Such a dreary thought did not stay with me long, as I dodged and weaved through the moving bodies—already dancing, yet the night was young. All those who passed shared a smile or a laugh. Half of them almost forgot to bow as I passed, though I hardly minded. A long-absent mirth was in the air, and to all it provided a freedom of expression—even myself.

I managed to get to my rooms, where Jacques stood, priming my costume. He did let out a small puff of relief at my appearance, which was painted on his face.

"Are you wearing makeup as well?" I asked, unable to keep a cackle from bubbling up at seeing a simple eyeliner on the old witch. Come to think of it, most of the staff downstairs were wearing varying degrees of makeup and a costume-like addition to their uniforms.

"Yes. I do not know how that human friend of yours managed, Thaddeus, but he has achieved a feat in this home I never thought possible. There is merriment! Even the staff are to be immersed in his fantasy." It seems that was all Jacques would offer as answer to my question.

I didn't speak, simply shaking my head as the smile remained on my lips. I undressed from my day clothes, a wary eye cast to the elaborate blue and black silks Jacques tended to. Neither of us spoke just then. I suppose neither knew what to say, fearing the once again darkened state that Jacques' truths had cast upon us.

Down to my undergarments and billowed shirt, Jacques helped me dress. Lavish and expensive fabrics made up my costume, the palate blue and black as forementioned. Deep blues were my britches and vest, both of which included far too many buttons and took us far too many minutes to figure out together. Next, a large black cloak was wrapped around my shoulders, which Jacques fastened with his old eyes glancing to my face.

Suddenly I was speaking, "Thank you, Jacques." Because of how silent the room had been prior, my voice seemed quite loud to my own ears. Jacques paused, looking forlorn for a moment. I pressed on, however, intending to free him to enjoy this night. "I did need to know."

He responded with a slow nod, giving a small *harrumph* as he tried to cover up the moistening of his eyes. "Perhaps I could have chosen a better day—"

"Today was better than a moment later. As my *mother's* heir..." I emphasized her title as that which I was, for the memory had more than proven this. "For her memory and my safety, I had to know—"

There was a knock at the door, and we spoke no more on the subject. Not even a moment was spared for Jacques to answer before Atlas threw the door open, much to both of our surprise. For Jacques, the initial shock came from the gesture being devoid of manners. This factor was not as significant to myself. I was more so surprised that the man stood before me in a large white, pink and golden robe, *a la francaise*, and had my jaw nearly to the floor.

"Do you like?" he chirped in glee and stepped into the room.

His hair was replaced by a black wig, piled on top of his head with a few ringlets falling down his neck. In hand was a white and gold lace-trimmed mask, fastened to a branch so it could be held up to his face. His face, beautifully painted, presented as incredibly feminine. I knew it was Atlas by scent, though if not for this heightened sense, I could have very easily mistaken him for a woman.

Jacques was speechless, his own mouth agape before he then instantly shut it, and his face was scarlet as he tended to my last few buttons. He then took his leave with a shuffle, giving two curt bows and mumbling, "Young lords, m-madam..." Flustered, he left the room.

Perhaps because it was Atlas, this grand entrance brought on a genuine laugh which danced from my belly. It was so true to who he was. I stepped forward as the door swung loosely shut behind Jacques, still laughing as I spun the human around.

"Oh, you are a treat, my dear," I stated, setting him down and gazing into those bright and life-filled eyes.

Atlas tittered along with me, taking no offense as he knew I didn't mean it as a form of mockery. "Well, I would hope," he giggled, nuzzling his painted face against my own. "I spent a good many late nights working on this!" He stated this proudly, spinning in a circle and clicking his heels along the floor.

He did look absolutely gorgeous, pulling another smile to my lips, my heart beating light and fast in affection. "You are divine," I hummed, pulling him close to me again. I drank up the sight of him while holding our bodies together, despite a few wiggles in objection.

"Oh stop, stop, stop! You loving little minx! You have an appearance to make, and if you ruffle my costume any further, I am going to be *very* cross with you," he threatened, though the excitement of my response was apparent in his eyes and did not falter.

"Yes alright," I responded softly, reluctantly letting him go. Seeing my hesitance, Atlas remained close, reaching up and adjusting my costume. He dusted off my shoulder and laid flat the lapels of my silk vest before wrapping the cape around me.

"The first of your guests have arrived and are enjoying the entertainment. I have it planned that you will make your appearance first, then Lady Evelyn...On another note," at this, his grin turned quite impish, "no stuffy fathers or their lot will be in attendance. Do hear me out before furrowing your brow like that!" Seeing my eyes widen, he waved off my concerns before they surfaced. "I won't bother you with the details, but they are having their own evening at my estate. My father is hosting, very exclusive...though they won't have nearly as much fun as we will, I guarantee." He chuckled, poking my brow. "Away with your scowl. Time to make merry!"

Despite my stirring anxiety upon learning of this new information, the events of the day had already exhausted me mentally. I simply could not focus on the details and decided to submit to the whims of the party. I sighed, giving a small nod and a lopsided smirk. "Let's make merry then," I agreed.

"Excellent!" Atlas turned to the mirror, adjusting himself quickly, and then took my arm, posing upon it like a prize. He dragged me through the door and down the hall. Due to the affliction of mental fatigue, I didn't fight him. The realization of what he was doing was delayed until we were rounding to the entrance of the ballroom. "Mask on!" the human swiftly mentioned, slipping an intricate black lace mask onto my face. Atlas raised his own to his face, and everything seemed to click a moment too late. The doors before us were thrown open, and the candlelight was nearly blinding.

Before I could react, the master of ceremonies demurely bowed his head and announced, "The young Lord Avalone and Lady Marquardt!" Beside me was Atlas, disguised as Evelyn.

A round of applause filled the hall. I was struck mute, as the ball was now upon us, and the rewards reaped. It was beautiful, vibrant and full of life—the likes of which having never filled these halls before. Hundreds, maybe even a thousand or more candles filled the space, from chandeliers or tiered pillars that surrounded the room. The warm, inviting glow cast upon the lawn I had seen earlier did not compare to this ethereal luminescence. Tables filled with decadent finger foods lined the walls, breaking only for small stages where contortionists, magicians or jugglers performed.

As the applause waivered, Atlas gave a small tug on my arm. Triggering the instinctual workings of my legs, we descended the stairs. A small giggle from Atlas bubbled up against my shoulder, my lover smirking up at me. "Oopsies," he cooed, obviously quite smitten with his little feat of trickery.

I cast a raised brow to the giggling imp on my arm, shaking my head but grinning. At the bottom of the stairs now, I gave Atlas a little spin, nimbly weaving us onto the dance floor. We were appropriately spaced but joined in with the other dancing couples. I teased, "What a mistake to be made...would be an absolute scandal should it be found out..."

"Best to stay quiet about the whole thing then, shouldn't we?" Atlas—masquerading as 'Evelyn'—purred with a small smile.

As we swayed, more attendees were announced here and there, though none warranted a full stop as our entrance had. My eyes could not leave my alleged fiancée, but his own attention was drawn to the entrance, and another trickster grin graced his face. This did pull my attention up the stairs, to the next couple announced.

"Mister Atlas Charron and Miss Agatha Dravenstebt!"

The couple at the top of the stairs was quite convincing as to who they were portraying, and they were dressed in slightly less extravagant costumes than my partner and myself. They descended the steps without much fanfare, their eyes locked quite affectionately on each other. We floated from the dance floor to intercept the couple, amused little giggles coming from the dame upon my arm. The reason was plain only to ourselves and the couple we approached.

Evelyn bowed before us, pretending to be Atlas, and the actual Atlas curtsied, the four of us in stitches at the whole situation—perhaps of relief, though with delight as well. Evelyn wore a proper suit accessorized with a long red cape, matching lace mask and a wild blonde wig. Anyone not in on the ruse would see the heir of the Charron family escorting Miss Agatha Dravenstebt, who also wore a complementary red gown.

"Good evening, Lord and Lady, and congratulations on your engagement." Evelyn hummed with a glint of mischievousness in her gaze. "The venue and atmosphere are marvelous...absolutely exquisite!" Thankfulness was evident in her tone, the candlelight and colors of the room dazzlingly reflected in her excited eyes.

Atlas returned the curtsey, lashes batting, "Thank you," he chirped. He, too, embraced his role in an incredibly convincing act.

Even Agatha—as herself, unlike the two actors beside us—bore a sincere smile. She was pleased with the situation and wore a rare expression. Happiness. An obviously well-thought-out plan between the three of them had been executed flawlessly, and I suspected her hand provided some magic assistance to achieve that end.

"You three truly are a force unmatched," I said with a guffaw, looking between the three of them with a shake of my head.

"We could not tell you," my lover cooed on my arm, giving it a squeeze and nuzzling in. "You simply would have worried yourself to death. Wouldn't he?" Atlas asked the other couple, who were quick in my betrayal and immediately nodded.

I held my chest, displaying how they wounded me with their words. Though just as the three conspirators beamed, the elation could not be kept from my face, nor laughter from passing my lips. For the night was young and drinks, food and merriment were bountiful for ourselves and our mirthful guests. The absence of fathers or other morose and unsavory family members allowed us the freedom to go into the evening and purely enjoy our night of celebration.

CHAPTER 16

Never had such jubilation rang through the halls of this frozen and crypt-like manor. Couples spun like twirling flowers in a child's hand, the ballroom seeming to have a heartbeat, and everyone moved in its rhythm. Other couples paired off, snuggled up in shadowed corners of the hall, or their presence evaporated entirely from the party. The mirth and chatter easily flowed like the drinks and musicians who scattered throughout the hall. In a state of *joie de vivre*, this party was a success, filled with quirky and upbeat melodies that fueled the enchanted humors of all.

Atlas, Agatha, Evelyn and myself joined every dance. Skirts and capes twirled with laughter as we spun. In a joyful stupor, the hours passed, and even when fatigue rendered me from the floor to rest in a chair, I was enraptured, continuing to observe the party.

From a tray passing by, I lifted off a glass of champagne and drank from its bubbling contents, also enjoying a few strawberries perched in the middle of my table. Over the rim of my glass, I observed even Jacques swaying to the music, chatting with another servant. In fact, it appeared to be the feline maid, still unnamed to me. When last I saw her, she had fled my father's office in tears, bearing a bruised face. Tonight, she bore a bright grin and happily engaged in her conversation with Jacques.

'Atlas'—Evelyn, that is—and Agatha were holding one another and swaying. The real Atlas had parted from my side at some point to give some instructions or check on how the guests were enjoying their time, but from across the room, I saw him headed towards me now. Another easy smile came to my face, and I stood to meet him.

Atlas waved his hand, prompting me to remain seated. He weaved through the dancing couples and guests. His scent reached my nose before he did, smelling of champagne and chocolate-covered almonds. Blue eyes were locked upon me as he stalked, and once next to me, Atlas leaned down to whisper into my ear. "Wait ten or so minutes, and then head like you are going to the gardens but circle back to your rooms. Make sure you are not seen..." The human breathed softly against my ear, then slowly stood—hand and then fingers lingering at my shoulder—till I then knew he had gone.

I turned to watch him go, but Atlas' furbelows and skirts seemed to disappear into the pulsing and constant movement of this lively beast of bodies he created. A small chuckle escaped me, feeling the excitement and euphoria of the atmosphere. With my brain fogged by its enchantment, I did as I was told. After waiting my time, I stood and made my way across the hall.

Remaining in the shadows, dodging guests and ducking behind curtains, I disappeared from sight, having already been long forgotten earlier in the night. I covertly slipped out a door to the back courtyard, bathed in the light of the moon as sharp, crisp air seized my lungs. Its polarity from the party cleared my head of its high, and my breath crystalized as delicate, frozen smoke.

Still my human's heated words had my blood rushing in a torrent and my feet carrying me the roundabout way to reenter the building. Light-footed I walked, with each step bringing another chilled breath and further clarity. The excitement of anticipated carnal touches waivered as an ever-present thought burst to the forefront of my perceptions. Blindly, as my vision was clouded with a wave of newfound guilt that washed over me, I slipped back into the manor and began to ascend the stairs with steady, quiet steps.

The once again unfolding guilt was from my own cowardice, from lacking the bravery to expose myself as I promised I would so many months prior. I allowed myself the happiness of his presence, touch and kiss, all while keeping such large and damning secrets from the human I so often called mine—the truth of what I am. I paused on a landing, gravity cementing me in place and my thoughts whipping about my skull like a typhoon. I could blame the considerable mental fatigue of the night and day leading to this moment, but in truth, it was always there. Only now I was ravaged by due guilt.

I could not take a single step forward, my inner storm consuming any muscles' capability and violently throwing my deceptions in my face. Vacant and empty was my existence before Atlas, for his bright and rhapsodic personality cleared the darkened clouds that haunted me. I bathed in it, enjoyed every moment while ignoring what I knew could possibly result in its end. How much I disgusted myself in this suddenly crashing moment—for what I had been considering love, was instead my complete taking advantage of this human's light. Regardless of doing it without malicious intent, it had been done.

I caught my reflection then, in the tall, curved windows that lined the walls of this staircase, my hand gripping the railing at the sight. My mother's hair, skin and eyes were reflected back at me. I was her child, her heir—but not hers alone. My angular face, well-built frame and even my thin lips were of my paternal heritage. In my reflection, I could see every inch that looked like my father, and I knew my conduct with Atlas up till now was exactly how he would selfishly act—all pleasure, no honesty.

With gritted teeth, energy surged up from my gut and into every extremity. I turned up the remaining stairs, decided that I would not continue down this path of deception. Perhaps it wasn't the best time, I thought, reaching the top of the stairs and turning down the hall. In the afterglow of such a victorious evening for the four of us...But then again, when would the timing be right? Would I ever truly experience happiness and bliss in its entirety with Atlas, if this truth rotted me from the inside out while I awaited an elusive proper moment?

I paused for a moment at my bedroom door, hand hovering over the brass doorknob, eyes locked on the wood grain of the ornate door. I rested my forehead against it, ears perking as I heard the human on the other side. Knowing Atlas, he likely was perched on the bed in some state of undress, trying to keep his breath slow, despite a racing and aroused heart.

I could hear him preening himself, likely catching glimpses in the mirror to make sure his blonde hair was swooped back and his pose upon my bed was seductive. One more selfish moment, I allowed myself. I smiled sadly for what—with the opening of this door—I anticipated would be lost. So I listened to his breath, heart and effervescence for this one more selfish moment.

My body moved like it was being controlled by marionette strings. More than anything, I wished this were not required of me, yet the circumstances demanded it. Two knuckles tapped the door, hand sinking down to the brass knob. It almost felt as if I were separating from my body, watching myself push the door open.

"Atlas?" I called out, head peeking around the corner.

As anticipated, my human was modeled upon my bed, the sight of him absolutely arresting. His costume lay in various discarded piles around the room, leaving him nearly bare. A chemise, detailed in lace, was falling off his shoulders and rolled up to his thighs. Depthless blue eyes brightened as I entered the room and hungrily ate up the sight of me as I closed the door, leaning back against it. He paused, however, the ravenous smirk turning down into a worried frown. My sad composure gave away my mood.

"Thaddeus? Is everything alright?" he asked, crawling to the edge of the bed. Breathtaking even in his worry, stray blonde hairs fell into his face, and his chemise billowed open, exposing his collarbone and chest.

Puppet strings pulled me forward, numb hands reaching out before me and holding his warm, flushed face. I didn't answer him at first, slowly running my thumbs against his cheeks and letting out a shaky breath. "We...I need to tell you something, Atlas..." My words chilled the air, and I had to suppress a fearful tremble.

Frown deepening, his hands came up to hold mine. Then he pulled them to his lips, kissing the knuckles of my fists. He pulled me down to the bed, having me sit and tucking his legs so he could, too. Lips still lingered on my knuckles, and with his voice barely above a soft breath, Atlas urged, "Then tell me, I am here..."

I watched as the blood ran from my face. Lip trembling, I could only muster a weak squeak. My heart raced, throbbing in pain from the drowning wave of anxiety that held me prisoner. I could not meet his worried eyes, staring at Eikþyrnir and the small glint of the room's candlelight she caught.

"There are things...Truths of me that you do not know, Atlas..." I began my confession, voice cracking. "I cannot continue keeping them from you, as it is not fair to you, and it is truly poisoning me too...Yet—" I gasped for air, tightly holding his hands in mine. *I am so fucking terrified to lose you,* I screamed in thought, shaking as I knew that it would be my reality in a mere moment.

In this moment of calamitous collapse and the seeming end of my life, this alluring and glowing human was laughing. "Oh, my sweet lord, you truly put your every worry before a thought, don't you?" He teased, giggling and leaning in to kiss my cheek.

"Please, I..." I tried begging him to listen. My certainty in this painful decision was crumbling at his smile.

"It hasn't occurred to you that in all these months...in any number of the times..." Atlas devolved into a fit of pleased and delighted giggles. He leaned back, one hand holding his belly as his gut busted through his words, "Any of the times we have been together...that I know and have always known?" His cheeks burned red as he shook with rapture.

I was stunned into silence, snapping back into my body and regaining my own point of view once more. It happened so quickly, my mind and limbs were numb trying to catch up with the rest of my conscious. I was all but incapacitated by it for a few seconds. Meanwhile, the human's laughter did settle, and he grinned, adjusting so that he was on all fours. He reached out to me again. One of his hands held up my wrist, and the other grabbed the silver circlet on my thumb and began to pull it off.

"D-Don't!" I begged, but it was too late.

The connection with Eikþyrnir was broken as she was pulled from my hand. Now, she was being twirled on Atlas' index finger. My body seemed to vibrate, the illusion magic that projected my mundane appearance fading with her removal. My eyes blinked back to their bright amber, and my tail sprouted and curled behind me. Aghast, my jaw dropped open, fangs pointing along with my ears. I froze in terror, unable to breathe or move.

"*De toute beauté...*" he whispered, wide-eyed and mesmerized by my appearance.

My frozen exterior melted as his small, kind hands held my face. Sitting before him on this bed, exposed for what I was, his reaction opposed everything I had ever been taught to expect. His attentive, loving nature did not falter at the sight of me. Instead, his beautiful, freckled face leaned in as his lips captured mine in a deep kiss.

My every muscle relaxed at his touch, his unwavering love washing over me in a tepid, enveloping wave. I pulled him to myself and buried my hands in his wild, blonde hair. Famished for each other, our tongues intertwined—breathing forgotten, for only the taste of each other was needed. Safe and cradled in his hands, every emotion and symptom that had built up till this moment were released. A small, choked-back sob caught and burned in my throat, tears slipping down my cheeks and blurring my vision.

"*Shhh,*" Atlas soothed, kissing each tear away. Like the delicate notes of a wind chime, his giggles poured forth, brushing back my hair and giving my face a small shake. "I *knew,* you silly creature. Oh and how I thought you did, too...Though I see that was obviously not the case!" He hummed to me sweetly, a few warmhearted guffaws making his exposed shoulders bounce.

"How?" I croaked, my vocabulary and capability of speech for the moment limited to single syllables.

More giggles erupted from him, tickled as he relished the situation. Getting comfortable, he lifted his slip and straddled my lap, arms rested and extended out over my shoulders. Then he curled his hands up against the back of my skull, fingers dancing along my hairline as he spoke.

"My family are a sort of...*secret keepers*," he sighed, settling on my lap and kissing along the bridge of my nose. "We are a human sect whose duties lie in keeping secrets and certain information safe from the general population by whatever means necessary—preventing hysteria, genocides or war, for that matter..." He stated this casually, waving it off as a simple thing, despite the life-altering information that it was.

Catching sight of my completely dumbstruck face—as I was without words at this revelation—with another laugh, he held my cheeks in his hands, squishing them. "Our allegiance lies with our kind, humans, and making sure of the powers of those...not human...do not abuse and extort the people." He smiled waggishly, amused with my residual shock to this enlightenment. "Not that we just go about *sharing* this information freely, of course...but my family is one of the more well-known in London."

Energy swelled up within me. Attempting to find words, finding the ability to move, I sprung up. Atlas tumbled onto his back, squealing in revelry as I descended upon him, wrapping my body around his. Hugging him, my tail oscillated back and forth in pure joy, rocking us against the bed.

"I didn't—had no clue—" I gasped. Gazing down at him, my hands were on either side of his face as further tears welled up, cleansing my soul of its guilt and fear.

Loving hands reached up to my face, wiping my tears with tender touch. "I see now. *Shhh*," he cooed in reassurance, doing what he could to quiet my blubbering. "Both of us made assumptions, it would seem...Just let me hold you, my foolish dear."

He hummed, pulling me to his breast, abundant kisses placed upon my crown. His heart ticked along in his chest, his breath slow and even between every kiss. I calmed against him, my face buried, nose pressed to the cloth upon his chest and trying to match his breath. We lay with our limbs intertwined and connected to one another. Grounded to each other, we stayed like this for several minutes. Atlas continued placing languid kisses on my scalp, finally sighing with a soft chuckle.

"To know you were risking everything to confess your truth makes my heart fill with even more love for you..." he whispered.

I raised my head, lip still trembling as I responded. "It would be the worst betrayal of our love, should I have never told you...and you were unaware...My heart couldn't bear it anymore. I couldn't deceive you—"

Atlas shook his head, eyes rolling and kissing me into silence. He pulled away for a breath, whispering to me as his hand delicately traced the tip of my pointed ear, "You are forgiven." Without a second thought, this amazing being—my human—exonerated me while pulling my bottom lip between his. "Though not for long, if I am left *wanting* in this bed..." he added heatedly.

I remembered now that he was scantily clad, as his body arched against mine. Lifelong tailored inhibition was abandoned with ease, and a pleased growl bubbled up in my throat as I dipped my lips to his neck, kissing his exposed flesh. A dyspneic moan left him, head stretching away and giving me a further canvas to lavish. I drew my fangs along his sweet skin, another pleased moan escaping him as goose flesh rose and fell along his arms. Blindly, his hands roamed over me, undoing and removing accessories of my costume. They joined his garments on the ground, haphazardly tossed aside without another thought.

Exhausted, we collapsed against the bed. Every inch of our bodies was tingling, hypersensitive as we panted into the other's faces. Atlas' eyes were barely open, weakly trying to kiss along my jaw. He seemed so fragile below me, and I dropped my head down, nuzzling him affectionately. I smiled, body humming as an afterglow of deep, rumbling purrs vibrated in my chest.

Atlas nestled his face against my own, smiling too in his state of fatigued bliss. "So cute..." he whispered, sliding his hand up my face to my large ears, then running his thumb over the pink flesh.

My sounds of bliss doubled, and I lowered my face against his breast, kissing his damp skin tenderly. Drained, I simply couldn't move, spare to wrap my arms around him. My eyes fell shut and succumbed to his deft fingertips caressing my large wolf ears, tiredly pointed out to the side.

CHAPTER 17

"Thaddeus... *Thaddeus!*" Atlas was shaking me, whispering sharply into my ear to rouse me from my slumber. He was swaddled in a robe, hair damp and braided to the side. Atlas must have risen while I slept, to clean and make himself decent. *"Thaddeus,* someone is at the door!" he hissed, a tinge of worry on his freckled face.

Rapid, feverish knocking at the door finally struck me, and with a bolt of energy I jumped a little, my attention snapping to the door. Large, white ears popped up on my skull, and my eyes widened in a moment of panic.

"For the sake of the gods, you two *open the door!*" Shocking to us both, it was the voice of Agatha on the other side.

I scrambled to find something to redress into—or anything decent really, being that I was still naked. My heart hammered in my chest. I was confused, yet relieved, yet again concerned for the reason for her appearance. Atlas, proving yet again to have a more controlled head on his shoulders during pressing moments, tossed my discarded britches from the floor to me. He walked over to the door and began to unlock it. Opening it a small crack, he peeked out and started to speak in a warm, playful purr, "Darling, we are a little busy—"

"Let me in," I heard her whisper sharply and place her hand on the door.

For a moment Atlas paused, glancing my way, for I was barely a leg into my britches and still appearing non-mundane. She huffed, pushing forward anyway as her magic sparked out over the door in a sage green color—the human easily pushed back as the magic shimmered over him as well. I had just managed to snatch the fabric up and began buttoning myself in as she closed the door behind her, hand placed on it once again and mumbling to herself. She was casting a spell.

"Agatha...what—" I began but was quickly cut off.

"Shut up, *SHUT UP!*" she hissed, not caring about my state of undress, nor exposing her craft to Atlas.

Her green eyes were demoralized and full of fear, and seeing this, I was immediately frozen in place. Something was *very* wrong. She turned back to the door, mumbling in tongues I did not recognize, finishing whatever spell she was casting. Atlas fell into my side, holding me and looking confused. For the moment, his own concern began to take hold of him.

When Agatha finished her spell, she threw the door back open, slamming it against the wall and rushing through the threshold. The door no longer opened to the hall of my wing in Avalone Manor, but rather to a black, seemingly formless void. Atlas and I watched in stunned silence. Sluggishly, the void began to take a shape. It was a small, unlit room, and the witch rushed about it, mumbling in her foreign tongue, which seemed to be igniting candles from order alone.

"Agatha, what on earth—" Atlas began as I had, but the red-haired woman rushed back to the door, cutting him off.

"No time to explain!" She threw two canvas bags at us, eyes

burning. "Dress and pack! I can only keep these spaces connected for a few minutes more!"

Suddenly, my bedroom echoed with loud banging—like the door was being slammed against, an attempt to breach. The spectral sounds of the door handle being rattled back and forth split the air, before once again the door was being thrust against by a body. I felt the color drain from my face, and Atlas mirrored this.

Agatha rushed back from the little room into my bedroom then. She threw drawers open and collected clothes into a third bag. "Dress warm, bring any papers...Leave anything else that can't be sold...*MOVE!*" she ordered Atlas and me.

Both of us had been frozen, staring at her with mouths agape. Fueled by our fear and the booming echo on the door from the hall that it was no longer connected to, we blindly changed, not sparing the time to button or fasten. Atlas finished dressing first and snatched up a bag. He quickly threw in the few items of his in the room before peeling away to the ensuite and collecting items there.

There wasn't a moment to think or to ask further questions—only to do as told. I collected Eikþyrnir from my nightstand, along with the small quantity of coins and other jewelry I had in the room. I turned next to my desk, pulling out papers for travel, blindly shoveling it all into my bag. All of this was done with loud banging filling the room, as well as the creaking of a door which this room was no longer connected to.

"We need to leave *NOW!*" Agatha shouted again, snatching two coats from my closet. Her arms were full as she ran through the threshold into the small, summoned room. Dropping those items to the floor, she turned back again to the door. Both hands were placed on it, mumbling her spell to undo the connection.

Atlas ran out, hooking his arm in mine and dragging me backwards into the small, dimly lit room. Hardly with both feet in, Agatha pulled the door shut behind us. From this side, I saw it was carved with intricate runes, unlike anything that could be found in the Avalone manor. We now were in a completely different building.

Agatha reached out, slamming her hands against the carved door. The wood splintered and cracked under them, bowing inwards as it was pushed from the other side. We, too, dropped all the items we held and ran back beside her, leaning our weight into it and helping to keep it shut.

"Do it!" Atlas shouted.

"By the power of the Eastern Wind, I order this connection severed!" Agatha screamed.

Her magic webbed out over the door, igniting like gunpowder with a loud crack. The three of us were thrown back from the force of it, and the few candles that had been lit were snuffed out, drowning us in darkness. The lingering sound of my father shouting disappeared with a rush of wind.

After these high-speed, terrifying moments, the dark that surrounded us was absolutely deafening in its silence. There were only the sounds of our thundering hearts and trembling breaths as we untangled. Blinking a few times, the stars that were caused by the burst of light were herded from my vision. I could then see around me. Though we were in morning hours, I saw as clearly as if it were the middle of the day. My own vision in the black of night was like that of a cat's, and thus all was clear. I could see the extent of the explosion's rampage. Shelves that lined the walls, which had been full of herbs and other natural medicinal items, were now shattered and spilled all over underfoot. We were in a small, single-room shack, appearing to be a workshop that could also serve as a dwelling for its owner.

"Are you both alright?" Atlas finally groaned, managing to stand up and dust himself off.

Agatha let out a small whimper, barely sitting up, hands trembling in front of her. They were covered in blood, with splinters sticking jaggedly out of the soft flesh of her palms. "M-More or less..." she voiced.

I responded with a simple assured grunt to Atlas, as any bruising was already mending and healing. More importantly, I stood to pull a toppled chair over to Agatha, then helped her into it. She sharply inhaled, and I could see her ankle jutting out to the side, likely dislocated. She waved her hand, another hiss of pain leaving her from the movement. The hearth sparked to life, albeit weakly, at her command.

"It's great that you can see in the dark, Thaddeus, but could you use that to light some candles, so we can too?" she asked, head gesturing to the sputtering fire. Agatha then let out a pained breath as she leaned back in her chair.

"O-Of course..."

I turned away with my instructions, numb to do anything else. Instructions, orders—these were good. I could be helpful and not stand with my mouth hung open. I located a candle and lit it, turning others upright along the way that had fallen due to the explosion. Once he could see, Atlas helped by crouching down next to Agatha.

"Oh, love..." he cooed, seeing her damaged state. "Is there anything...I can do?"

He, too, followed her instructions as she pointed to a closet in the corner and uttered two short words, "Medical kit."

Glancing out the single window, I saw that the glass was newly cracked but holding. We no longer were in the city, but rather, the wilderness. This small dwelling was surrounded by towering conifers and deep drifts of snow, nestled against a mountainous wall of earth. The only natural light came from the moon above, casting her cool glow over the landscape.

Atlas, meanwhile, had returned to Agatha's side. He rummaged through the bag of supplies, then turned and addressed the wounds on her hands, ridding them of splinters. Though rattled too, my human was much more capable at the moment than I was, able to think and address matters with functioning thoughts. The witch silently writhed in her seat, eyes remaining closed while the human worked as delicately as he could.

I pulled another chair close, sitting before her and waiting for more orders. My head was numb, shut down to any thought of my own. Questions were beginning to form in my skull, but I could not create words to ask them.

"Thaddeus," I turned to Atlas' benign voice and found his blue eyes locked onto his work. He glanced down to Agatha's ankle, jutted out at the wrong angle, and bit his lip. "Her ankle is dislocated... You're going to have to set it."

His voice was mellow and comforting, but still authoritative. A pang of desire to be back in our bed—tangled in each other's limbs, blissful and oblivious—hit me. It had to be shrugged off though, for our friend was hurt and in pain. She sure as hell couldn't do it herself. I mustered a nod in response to Atlas, who had managed to remove the last splinters and was bandaging her hands.

Despite her tremendous pain, Agatha was coherent, as evidenced by her barking voice, "Give me something to bite down on. Don't need to lose my tongue."

In my still numbed state, her order was complacently followed. I grabbed a leather belt and folded it twice, then offered it to her.

The witch clamped her teeth down, already being held back by Atlas. He hugged her tightly from behind, blue eyes focused down to me. When he nodded, I stooped down, observing for a moment. I knew what I must do.

Agatha screamed through the leather, teeth bared and sunken into it. It was a quick, wet sound as I snapped her ankle back into place, but it was not broken, and that seemed like a small victory.

"Fucking *assholes!*" she seethed, the belt falling from her mouth. She writhed again in pain but held to consciousness with an iron grip, the effort dampening her brow with sweat. She was mended for the time being, practically hissing as she drew in shuddering breaths to calm herself, holding her belly. "Bruised ribs too. Fuck..."

Atlas fluttered around, looking to keep working. I just couldn't bear it—neither being away from his side nor how his constant movement was overstimulating. This is why I reached out and pulled him close. I was sitting already, and he stood next to me. He could not remain still enough to take a chair and sit, nor were there any chairs for him to do so. His small hands settled for running through my hair. In this way, he could keep moving, and I could settle. That was good enough for the moment.

The small hearth sputtered and cracked, but otherwise we sat in silence, absorbing the situation and waiting to find out just what had happened. My questions quickly turned into dozens, all posed on my tongue and ready to rapidly fire. The pair of us were staring, and when Agatha's eyes opened to see this, she growled—this time in frustration.

"Your cousin, the little black-haired lass? Verona, is it?" she asked.

I blinked, trying to remember English. I nodded and then titled my head in curiosity, wondering what she had to do with any of this.

"Congratulations," she wheezed sarcastically. "The true Avalone heir has presented as an alpha."

"That isn't good," Atlas stated bluntly. Surely, he did not know every in and out, but by his statement alone I figured that he knew some. His words mirrored what mine would have been anyways, if they would only pass my lips.

"I do not know everything, but I can tell you what I do...We will go from there," Agatha stated. The pain in her ribs was going to keep this short and to the point. My hand slid up to Atlas' which rested on my shoulder, intertwining with his as the witch continued. "Some gathering of your family happened, their own celebration of this engagement. Word has it that the little pup alpha rolled a maid during some activity." The witch groaned, sitting up a little more, and it helped with her breathing. "Which is apparently all that was needed for her mother to declare she is to be made regent of the district. Bold bitch..." She commented offhandedly. "In any case, a huge fight ensued, wherever the fuck they were..."

Atlas squeezed my hand tightly, for they had been at his father's estate. Agatha continued, "So your father leaves there and shows up to the masquerade—which had practically turned into an orgy shortly after you slinked off..." I felt myself pale in color, about to faint at the thought, and Atlas pulled me tightly against him, grounding me. "He starts ordering the staff to find you. 'Execute the plan,' is what he said." Agatha paused there, like she was thinking, trying to remember what came next. "Then, the butler... tall and dark? The one who follows you everywhere, like an overbearing shadow."

I nodded, miraculously finding my ability to speak. "Jacques."

"Yes," she confirmed. "He grabs Evelyn and I...and just zaps us with memories or something."

I couldn't help as my face fell flat, lips pressing thin. To use magic like that so openly and suddenly...I felt my guts burn, for I had known he was holding back something, yet I had not pressed. Agatha's own face was pinched with worry, but she never had been one to soften a blow, and now was not going to be the first time. Seriousness overtook her face.

"It turned to chaos. Your father had..." She shivered, recalling. "He had that clerk of his with him—he's a goddamn necromancer, smelled of black magic. The two of them just started slaughtering people, collecting for a blood magic, and the butler...Jacques, he zapped us because he knew..."

"What?" It was Atlas who spoke up, his voice dry and expecting.

"Your father was executing a plan to transfer souls, his and yours. He wanted to take your body, because he thinks you're some *god?*" She wheezed skeptically, almost asking in disbelief. It seemed as though she did not believe whatever information had been planted by Jacques.

"*What?*" Atlas squawked. His mouth hung open, befuddled. My lips remained thin and pale.

Agatha's brow furrowed. They weren't her memories, but they were planted in her mind for the need of enlisting her help. "No..." she corrected. "I think...your mom was. So you're a sort of demigod. Technically?" Seeing our floundering, shocked faces, she quickly shot off what she knew, foreseeing the questions that were to come. "Your good ol' father thinks you are too, and if he can have your body as his own, he can keep his position..." Agatha's words faded away.

She's something more. The thought echoed in my head as it had so many times before. I had only learned she was a god—a minor god—about half a day before the other two did. In my shock, I was dense and had not fully connected what that also meant. For during that time, it did not occur to me that any of the wonderful gifts she possessed, and Jacques had mentioned, would be inherited by me. The elusive, missing piece of the puzzle was known and now completed the picture. Any question I had ever conjured up had an answer now.

Why does he despise me? Answer, I reminded him of what he cut his losses on. *Why does he terrify me?* Answer, he sought to wear me down so he could take my body...*Why marry me off to a beta?* Answer, he desired her. I was unlikely to have children, but if he was in my body, then he could produce a spare vessel.

I could hear the human and witch talking—bickering, actually. Some of it managed to soak into my exhausted brain. Jacques gave these memories to Agatha and Evelyn to help me escape. For the grim's immediate safety from the necromancer, Jacques took Evelyn with him. However, the butler was going to be targeted first, since my father knew his allegiance lay with me. If they did manage to track him down, at least I wouldn't be with him.

The rest we knew: Agatha had saved our lives, transported us here, and here we had to wait. We had to hope that Jacques and Evelyn were not found. We were left to pray, to hope. Somehow, we would need to come up with how to leave England's shores—and do so still breathing.

CHAPTER 18

All of us were exhausted. Not to mention, the witch was also battered and bruised. I was numb and unable to focus. For the moment, though, we were safe—smuggled away and hidden in a 'hunting cabin' which belonged to the witch's family. It was a small, one-room building with a single door and window. It had one bed, big enough for two, which seemed to be the intended maximum capacity of the whole cabin. Agatha's magic kept the fire crackling, so it was hospitable, despite the thick blanket of snow outside. The decision was easily made for us to rest and see what the morning would bring.

We tried to coax Agatha to take the bed, but she firmly insisted on sitting upright in her chair—claiming she would not get any sleep due to her rib pain anyways. I was nearly senseless from over-stimulation, as a result of our situation. Therefore, I did not argue. Yet even through my clouded mind, I understood that she would get no sleep while she worried about Evelyn—injured or not.

Atlas steered me to the bed, peeling back the quilts and navigating me into it. He then followed, snuggling up to my chest and pulling the blankets over us. Instinctually, I wrapped my arms around him and held him protectively. He did not fight or tease.

Instead, he clung to me. His small hands pressed to my chest and his nose under my chin.

"We will get through this..." he assured me.

My heart squeezed painfully in my chest, longing for the humor and sultry bliss we had only a few hours prior. My tail wrapped around his waist, a shuddering sigh wracking my body as we curled together. Fear and anxiety tightly held me in their desolate palms. Our future days were saturated with it, and the notion was terrifying. My dismal thoughts fizzled as the human pressed a grounding kiss to my throat, and I found words for response. My own lips tenderly kissed his brow and smoothed back his wild blonde curls.

"Together...together we will." That was all that needed to be said, and it was plain to see that was how we would manage to survive.

~

Somehow, we all managed to fall asleep at various points during the night, though it was restless. We were all paralyzed by the recent, horrifying events. Atlas and I clung to one another, while Agatha remained in her seat. The faint crackle of the hearth and the slow-moving projection of moonlight from the sole window told us of the hours that passed us by. Well into the morning hours we lay so. The world around this cabin continued to move on, while we remained statues.

That was, until the doorknob turned, and the splintered door opened to two bundled figures in the snow. A snarl began to rip from my throat, hair standing on end. On pure instinct, I was about to charge the entrance when Agatha's shouting cut me short.

"Evey!" the female witch shouted, tears springing to her emerald eyes as she hobbled up from her post.

A small wail escaped the smaller of the figures, and my fiancée tossed back her hood, hair loose and whipped back from the wind as she rushed to embrace her partner. "Thank the gods!" she began, and her arms wrapped quickly around the bruised redhead. "Agatha, you're injured..."

The grim was silenced as the witch heatedly kissed her, not letting the younger go despite her obvious discomfort. "Just some bumps and bruises, my love...Having you in my arms again is all I need right now!" The women cried and worried over each other, and the vacant look that Agatha's eyes had held throughout the night now washed away.

Atlas and myself rose from the bed, and Atlas nimbly wrapped his arms around me, a small smile of relief on his face at the women being reunited. The second cloaked figure closed the door and pulled back his own hood, unloading his burdens to the floor. He looked around the cabin, wrinkling his nose at the state of chaos we had left it in after last night.

Atlas squeezed me a little tighter, stiffening in nerves, because he did not recognize who it was. Reassuringly, I hugged the human back, nuzzling the top of his head. I knew who it was, for his scent had not changed. "Jacques..." I managed to mutter.

The witch smiled at the mention of his name and stepped toward us. His own worry melted from his changed face at the sight of us. His hair was now raven-black in color. Even the texture was different, as it was wavy and bounced against his stubbled chin. The most striking change—and biggest culprit for Atlas' inability to connect our ally and the man before us—was his regression in age. Hardly appearing out of his twenties, all age lines were absent.

"Lady Evelyn informed me of your relationship." Even his voice had changed, and a French accent was now on his tongue. "I will say, it comes not as a surprise to me..." He wrapped his arms around us, sighing as he squeezed us tightly. "How glad I am to see you safe."

Atlas wiggled against this—strange to him—man, his blonde brows pinching together as the witch embraced us. "He's about a lifetime younger—" Atlas began to protest.

Relieved as the stress of this limbo subsided, I doubled over in laughter, holding my sides. Atlas and Jacques both gained worried looks at my fit, but still I gasped for air and held my reddening face.

"H-He is a witch, an old one at that," I explained, arms reaching for my mate and pulling him to me. Small giggles bubbled up as I shook my head. With Jacques here, I was relieved, and it washed over me like a warm, refreshing bath. "We all have one, really." I said this with a nod to Evelyn and Agatha. Master and servant, a bond of protection.

Atlas rolled his eyes in realization, letting out his own chortle of relief before clapping Jacques on the back. "Oh I see, well I am the least educated out of the five of us, I suppose. I did not know your lot could so drastically change yourselves—how very convenient for our situation!" The human's infectious glow had returned to his cheeks, smiling bright and beautifully for the first time since our departure from my home.

I realized with complete and absolute clarity for the first time in my life, that place never had been a home. Rather, it was but a prison to my life thus far. A home was where one felt loved, wanted, and had a sense of belonging. Here in this chaotic, small cabin, surrounded by snow-covered trees in the middle of nowhere—Agatha embracing Evelyn, Atlas reaching up and smooshing around Jacques' face—in all their presence, this was the closest I had ever been to a home. *They* were my home, and at the center of that, of my world, was Atlas.

At this moment, I was the farthest I had ever gone from the grounds of Avalone Manor. I was breathing fresh air, and the chains that had long held me hostage were broken. Before meeting Atlas, I merely was existing, just barely. My life was seemingly predestined for the servitude and pleasure of my father—a service which slowly suffocated and subdued me, where I was only a doorframe away from losing my body and life.

Now, I was free, and I had the possibility of more for my life. Looking around at my friends and my mate, I felt the final garment of who I had been stripped away. Bare and ready to be molded anew, I was prepared for the adventure that my life could be.

I was in love—a deep and devoted love with a human who accepted me for all that I was. It was something I had only dared to dream of, a life cradled in his arms. The beings in this shack, along with a few canvas bags of possessions, may be all I had in this world—but that being said, I could not be happier with my lot. Despite the odds, I had created this for myself, and I could not ask for anything more.

Disrupting Atlas' conversation with Jacques, I leaned against him, pressing my face into his impossibly untamed hair. I closed my eyes and beamed in a state of true happiness. Despite being on the run, faced with filicide should my father capture me once again—I truly knew that the beings within these four walls were with me, and they were my heart. The human smiled, reaching up a hand and patting my own white head, a soft kiss pressed to my brow.

Atlas chirped, "So tell us, Jacques. You have gotten us this far— what's the plan for getting us off English soil?"

CHAPTER 19

Jacques

Rumors of the disaster at Avalone Manor remained the talk of London for weeks following. The manor and grounds were reduced to ashes from an alleged fire that had broken out, claiming the lives of dozens of party attendees, staff, and the young bride and groom to be. This is what the humans knew and whispered in the weeks after. It was a good cover story, as humans never do take well to mass murder at the hand of any supernatural beast, let alone a necromancer. Both the fire and later rumors may have had my own hand and wagging tongue of contribution.

For my many lives, I had generally stayed out of such matters, but driven by my affection for the young shifter—and my desire to see him prosper—I felt that the sooner this event was forgotten, the sooner then he could live. The first step to achieving this—one I found was going quite well, given that my former master was missing and wanted for questioning—was a manhunt, headed by the Reverend Marquardt. Wherever the vile tick was (even I could not quite locate him), it would not be his top priority to hunt down my charges.

The courts and circles of nonhumans were plagued by power

struggles, in addition to dozens of sudden disappearances and suicides. This was typical of sudden upheavals of power, and this too aided for the courts to be focused elsewhere. The quartet of youths and myself could hone our plan for leaving this country without the worry of discovery breathing down their necks.

The five of us lived in the sapphist's hideaway for nearly a month, which was just long enough for the red-headed witch to heal. Neither of us were well versed in healing magics, and thus it was impossible to move it along any faster. It came as a relief to me—for though I had never intended to meddle, I'd brewed possibilities for how I could over the years. No such trains of thought had ever planned for smuggling two, let alone *four*, people from these lands, however.

In comparison to the hunt for Thaddeus' father and by extent himself, the two women were hardly the subject of any rumors. Spare the raving reverend, whose preaching and claims died on the ears of humans once he was decided to be insanely obsessional. Both women were forgotten and thus could move ahead. They did so gladly, considering that their alternative was to remain in a cabin shared by another couple and myself, winter keeping us indoors, and alternate which couple could use the bed. My opinion mirrored theirs, as fewer beings in this dwelling would allow lesser a chance of someone thinking the home was occupied.

It was late February when the witch and grim decided they would leave for Ireland. Witches were well known for their loyalty to their masters, but their loyalty to family was something far stronger. Such was a positive result of the distasteful history of witch hunting and burnings. The redheaded one had extended relations who would without question house them, and so they made the decision to live with her family there.

The morning the women set out became a quite despondent affair. Sadness from his friends' departure darkened Thaddeus' soul. Whereas humans don't agree with me on the best of days, the one whom Thaddeus bonded to was of superior quality compared to those I had encountered during my lifetimes. The small shifter's mind did not dwell long in the dismal valleys of depression, for the human was radiance personified and uplifted Thaddeus from that dark place with kisses and affection. He spoke truths of how the men's own escape was far more perilous a venture and would endanger the others. Atlas further emphasized that this farewell was not a forever goodbye, and that surely as strong a friendship as they had cultivated would not wane with distance.

So the women left us, hand in hand, carrying packs full of essentials I had acquired from a nearby village for their travels. Their paths and story parted thereafter from our own. I am not a creature who has the sight of what the future holds, but I now know that this would not be the last time Thaddeus' path—or my own for that matter—would cross with theirs. It would, however, be many years before that would happen again. Over the rolling hills they walked, until with a small flash of green they disappeared—the witch's magic whisking them away from sight and my thoughts.

Those who remained were Thaddeus, his human and myself. There were enough stores of firewood, food items and books to last us through the remaining winter, as well as a variety of easily obtainable supplies should I take a few days to travel to the nearest village. It was a time of quiet and healing for them. The mornings were spent sleeping in each other's arms, settling into a domestic life with one another. Their nights were spent tangled and gasping for breaths, but I did not mind. Thaddeus was happy, and I only shared the space to cook for us all.

Truthfully, I enjoyed being able to sit in the nature surrounding this hideout, listening to the music of the wind through the trees and observing the world as time unraveled. This was how we rode out the weeks till spring came and passenger ships once more would leave the harbors to cross the sea. It was my suggestion—as was the goal of many conceived plans, though they had previously only involved Thaddeus—that he and his human would leave for the Americas.

My new appearance was a great advantage, and in the weeks before their leave I traded and sold the items of value that they brought with them on the night of their escape. On my own I effortlessly traveled to London, where the items sold at a premium when it was confirmed that they belonged to the late Avalone family. Such was a simple feat, with the notoriety of the fire and fall of the family fresh in the public's mind. Both supernatural and mundane beings alike find morbid trinkets with infamous backgrounds to be worth more than their weight in coin.

I sold it all—spare Eikþyrnir, as Thaddeus still needed her for their travels. After selling all else, both Thaddeus and the human were provided with two very full pouches of coins. It was more than enough to fund their journey, in comfort, over the sea. Then they could live for a good while on those funds alone, should settling or finding agreeable work prove to be challenging.

So there I stood, watching their ship slip away over the horizon. With Thaddeus and his human upon it, I felt my heart ache. The sun was high and bright in the sky, and the sea lapped at my feet. Sensations were barely felt, as my eyes were locked on the receding transport. I longed to be there for Thaddeus—*Tyler*, as his papers now said. Tyler Azuzels was the name he had chosen, the name he would bear from then on.

Somewhere along the years of my watching and caring for him, a longtime indifferent part of my being had begun to love once again. An emotion, somewhat stirred to a state of wakefulness by his mother, had bloomed to full life as he grew. I would spend decades regretting that I did not join him on that journey, gazing wide-eyed out over the sea to the world beyond, leaving the shores of the only land he knew behind.

Though it pained me and left me with regret, I knew I would only have hindered his growth. He needed to experience and live through the difficulties of what his lover had lost. Only by doing this on his own could he become the man he was destined to be. I watched as the first chapter of our lives took pause here, on the shores of England. On a beautiful day, full of possibility and light, he no longer needed my care or watchful eye. Finally, he was prepared to take and build his own life. The pain of him slowly pulling away from my reach was shattering, but I knew I must bear the burden.

This was not the end of his story, nor my own. Far from it, in fact. This was, however, the new beginning he deserved. I felt her presence for just a moment, on those shores—his mother, my dear friend, watched too as he disappeared from the horizon. She could finally rest peacefully as he left these waters and made his life anew. I would see him again, many years later. Then, our story—our love—would grow, would flourish. Heeding the human's advice from earlier, I held hope that although this was for now farewell, it was not our goodbye.

END OF BOOK ONE

GLOSSARY

Alpha — marker / hierarchy marker (see Appendix)

Angel — creatures born from Christendom (sometimes human in appearance) bearing large wings capable of flight

Anthropoid Mein — an appearance resembling that of humans in form, look or manner; slang term for human form or appearing human

Beast — slang term referring to any creature that can take a shape other than human

Beta — marker / hierarchy marker (see Appendix)

Breed — a specific type of creature that exists within a broader category; most successful procreation is done within one's same breed (example: werebeasts, skinwalkers and grims are breeds within the *shifter* classification)

Cardinal Dragons — the first four dragons (names: Ke'ahi, Kuki, Talahm and Calder) who control the four winds (Southern, Eastern, Western and Northern respectively); revered as gods in supernatural theology; are believed to have created all supernatural beings

The Craft — umbrella term used for any form of magic

Demigod — any child born of a major or minor god and someone not within that classification

Demons — the most diverse group of supernatural creatures, easily adaptable to their surroundings and capable of possessing a variety of unique characteristics; some have magical capabilities while others do not; abide by their own caste system

Dragons — creatures of mythology capable of taking on the shape of a human as well as a large reptilian shape of lore; have not been knowingly witnessed for several generations

Eikþyrnir — second ring that Jacques crafted from Josephine's necklace, which assists in maintaining a mundane appearance (Norse origin, meaning *stag that stands upon Valhalla*)

Garmr — a ring crafted by Jacques' magic, which assists with maintaining a mundane appearance

Grim — creature that takes the form of a large black dog; human lore tells of these creatures guarding over the cemetery of the church they are bound to

Incubus — a type of demon that feeds off of the sexual energy of its prey; human lore suggests these creatures are only male, though it is not actually gender-specific

Lîlît — referring to Lilith, first wife of Adam and the first she-demon; a slang term used for a false god

Lycan — term used by some to describe a werewolf

Mage — interchangeable term with *witch* for a user of magic, regardless of gender, who draws their powers from the earth or a deity

Magic Paralysis — a common (temporary) side effect of the use of magic on a non-magic-user's body or mind, wherein the non-magic-user is unable to move until the lingering magic in their system dissipates

Major Gods — gods who possess infinite power, reigning control over the universe and earth on grander scales; death is only possible at the hand of another major god or a weapon crafted by one

Minor Gods — gods who have limitations to their capabilities and powers which are finite; death is possible through natural, accidental or homicidal events

Mother — goddess of light and creator of life; created the first dragons; considered the most supreme being by many supernatural beings (excluding demons)

Mundane — a term used in the supernatural community that refers to humans

Omega — marker / hierarchy marker (see Appendix)

Pack — a group of being intimately affiliated with one another; a term typically referring to immediate or extended family, though they do not always need to be of blood relation (example: marriage will bind one to a new pack)

Shapeshifter — a creature capable of changing their shape to two or more different animal forms, able to change minor physical features (example: shape of ears)

Shifter — a slang term for any creature capable of changing their shape in any way

Skinwalker — a creature capable of changing their shape to two or more conceivable animal forms (includes the ability to take on the forms of other supernatural creatures or humans); able to alter physical traits with ease; most natural form is often a mix of features belonging to an array of animals

Species — an umbrella term for a category of creatures who can procreate and produce offspring with one another, though with potentially more difficulty than a mated couple within the same breed (example: dragons can change their appearance, but they are unable to procreate with any other *shifters*; therefore, they are considered their own species called *drake*)

Ursus — Latin word meaning *bear*

Werebeast — a creature capable of taking only one form besides their human appearance (variable phases possible); affected by the phases of the moon (example: werewolf, grim)

Witch — interchangeable term with *mage* for a user of magic, regardless of gender, who draws their powers from the earth or a deity

Wizard — magic-user whose powers come from magical items

APPENDIX

An Overview of the Supernatural Caste System

Most supernatural creatures abide a hierarchy wherein a creature will be born biologically male or female — this is one's *primary sex*. A supernatural being also possesses an additional *secondary sex*, which is determinable once the onset of puberty begins. There are three potential secondary sexes — alpha, beta and omega. These secondary sex hierarchy markers are most significant among creatures such as shifters, werebeasts and dragons.

Most family units (often referred to as a *pack*) consist of polygamous relationships among three individuals, one of each marker (alpha, beta and omega). Biological females or males can fall into any marker category, but general statistics are listed and further detailed below. More traditional families believe that the alpha's role is to lead, betas are meant to follow, and omegas should be taken care of as the alpha deems fit. This is a more archaic practice, rarely observed in the same fashion today. Regardless of marker, most modern creatures who find themselves within this hierarchy conduct themselves in such a way that all parties are equal.

Alpha

Generally, alphas have larger bulk and strong builds — capable of producing pheromones that can attract potential mates or impose younger, weaker creatures into submission. Statistics show that 80% of alphas will be males and 20% will be females. Alpha is the second most common hierarchy marker among supernatural births (beta is most common). Most old supernatural families believe that an alpha should lead their pack or family.

Male alphas are generally able to sire alpha females, beta females, or any omega. Alpha females are the rarest and most respected of any category. They are only capable of conceiving with an alpha male, and they are able to sire beta females, omega females, or omega males. The outward appearance of an alpha female is a strong, stocky build.

Beta

Betas have an equally likely chance of being male or female and have no additional or absent physical characteristics. This is the largest populated caste, given that creatures whose species do not observe this hierarchy are referred to as betas. Creatures who are not affected by pheromones are often referred to as betas. Able to stand up to an alpha or an omega, betas maintain an equal balance of power between all three partners. Beta males can only sire a beta female or an omega female (this is a rarer occasion). Beta females are capable of siring an alpha male, alpha female or beta male.

Omega

The least populated caste, omegas possess a rare marker and as such are coveted and often live pampered lives. Physical features include shorter stature and wide hips. Statistically, the omega demographic is made up of 90% females, and the remaining 10% are made up of either omega males (1-5%) or creatures who are intersex. Exact percentages are unknown for this portion of the omega class.

Omega females appear as typical females in terms of bodily functions and characteristics. They are able to become pregnant during any time of year, however this can still be met with difficulty. Omega females can only be sired with an alpha male, alpha female, or a beta male.

Omega males are the most exceedingly rare within this caste system. Their anatomy differs greatly from any other males within this caste. Males possess both male and female reproductive organs. Omega males are incapable of siring another. If consummation does result in a pregnancy, omega males will typically gestate the child to full term before having a cesarean section. In times past, male omegas would die during childbirth approximately 95% of the time, but advancements in technology have dramatically lowered those rates.

When it comes to intersex omegas, this least studied group of the caste is the most varied. From one creature to the next, circumstances are not the same. Consummation sometimes results in a new species—including but not limited to angels, ancient demons, gods, and demigods. An intersex omega may possess the reproductive organs (full or partial) of both sexes. Due to this, there is some overlap between intersex omegas and male omegas. Typically capable of both conceiving from another and being the sire, there have been a handful cases in which creatures reproduced by way of mitosis. Physical appearance is dependent on the individual.

ELI PRITZL is a nonbinary, first-time author living in northcentral Wisconsin with their fiancé and pack of large, fluffy dogs and two cats. Their heart truly sings when enjoying hobbies such as cosplaying, working with miniatures, reading and, of course, writing! Since adolescence, Eli has been drawn to folk, fairy and make-believe stories involving the supernatural. Readers will find their own interpretation of such tales reflected in *Amber Eyes* and other planned works.

They have received an associate's degree in arts and science from the University of Wisconsin – Marathon, as well as an associate's in accounting from Northcentral Technical College. Eli's goal for this series (and all their writing) is to provide representation for the LGBTQ+ community and those with mental and physical disabilities in romance fiction.